I0761871

† THE PASSION OF ADELIA

•

Maxime Norrvik

DREAMWICKS

Capel Sound, Victoria, Australia.
This is a work of fiction. Names, characters, businesses, places, events, locales, and incidents are either the products of the author's imagination or used in a fictitious manner. Any resemblance to actual persons, living or dead, or actual events is purely coincidental.

The Passion of Adelia / Maxime Norrvik – 1st ed.
A woman returns home as an undead to reclaim her life with her human boyfriend.
This book contains light erotic scenes and subjects of death and violence that may not be appropriate for some readers.
ISBN-978-0-6484349-3-1 (Hardback)

•

Dedication

I dedicate this work, first to my daughter Sephil, who is my guiding force in everything I do, and then to the great readers who will be reading it and be a part of the tragic yet human journey of one of my favorite characters. May many goblets of happiness feed your soul!

Oh no! To see him again, it doesn't matter where!
In heaven's oases or within a boiling vortex,
under serene moons or within purple horrors!

And to be with him every springtime
And winter, in one anguished knot,
around his bloody neck!

— Gabriela Mistral

The Passion of Adelia

1

A Sense of Me

I can see. Light enters my eyes. I can smell. The esters of flowers strum the cilia in my nose like guitar strings and stir my olfactory sense, but nothing like garlic to make me pick up my wings and check out of town. This is untrue but I like to say it. If you pinch me, I can feel pressure in my skin. I can sense temperatures, hot and cold. My somatic sensors are dull, yet operational.

I can hear a whimpering child five miles away—if I focus. I can think, hold a pen, jot notes, and connect the dots. I can devise ideas and plans. I have answers to problems and problems to answers and can cause chaos if I want. I don't have to know everything to be smart.

Water is dead to me. I can neither taste nor smell it, nor find a care for it. My revenant gustatory calyculi can taste the alcohol, anything pungent. My favorite drinks are brandy and tequila, and I don't mind enjoying them from time to time.

I have, however, a strong desire for blood. And there lies the answer to who I am, for still feeling, still thinking, still smelling and seeing. It is all gift of that life-giving nectar that feeds those infected with this virus and keeps souls between life and death.

It's the iron in the blood that gives the kinetic energy, the electricity, and keeps a body, that is otherwise dead, animated. It's what awakens my dead cells and makes my body shiver with passion when he touches me.

I can become a scentless, zero percent alcohol distillation that weaves undetected around a room. I can hide within the molecules of the air, become one with the air, with the wind. Even with my ability to connect the dots, this is incomprehensible. Let others do the science. In many ways I find my essence similar to lava, which is both liquid and solid, or to methane vapor that freezes in outer space.

To feed, though, I must become visible and tangible. I've found no way out of that. Mind, I have no joy in draining you, no love for you dying with suffering, scared—but even the dead must get their iron to keep their foot out of the grave, meander through the world, and not be prey.

I find interesting this desire to "not want to let go." Even departing souls cling to what little animation remains on their fleshy toes—like the spirit of the deer fights for its last breath in the savanna after the lion's bite. I understand. That little palpitation of life is dear, like the last little warmth from a fire during the grips of merciless winter. We try to squeeze the last bit of it. You want to clutch it, wrap it around you!

Love has its own beating heart, it's its own form of life. That is why it resists being torn from its foundation, why it fights its own death. Love's death is unhappiness. Love is a skin, and it has a home—the eyes of the one you love, while his heart, or her heart, is your earth. Within that earth, love is life. When that earth grows cold, love shivers and seeks warmth. It transforms into something that it was not before. For love is two sides of a coin. On one side, it is joy; on the other, it is tears.

It is these lives I deprive people of when I go on my hunts. You can see how they fight for their last breath—how they struggle so fevereshly to keep their candle burning! As I raise my jaw—filled with their warm blood—and stare at the moon, their lifeless or unconscious bodies are a testament to their failure in the fight. This is how I kill you.

To be fair, I give you life—sometimes. Turning you into one like me is not so evil unless *you* become evil. Evil is hate, it comes through it. Those who do not hate commit no evil. Hate is a clutch that will not release a spirit that should be free.

I do not kill with joy. I rather you die a peaceful death, one that will levitate you into whatever light or emptiness you desire. I let you be like me if you wish to die, out of pity, and pity is love. If you cannot enjoy life, then you can enjoy death.

Indeed, love is my ague, my killer. But suffering is life, and if I will live undead then so be it. There is another moon tomorrow. Whatever I felt tonight might disappear with the new midnight light.

For you see, I love. Yes, I love a man. But he doesn't know I am dead. He is the one I live for. He is the reason I drain you and make you suffer. The reason I exist! If he was gone, I would go with him. I'd dive into a pool of garlic and stakes and fire and end what ought to have ended the day I became a vampire.

2

My Puzzle

There is a danger in blood. Drink the wrong one, and you can become angry. Blood transmits the DNA of its bearer into your revenant veins. Through it, you drink the sorrow and the love. Sometimes, the hate. It all depends on its genetic wiring. It is perilous to be a vampire.

Of course, you do not become someone "different." You don't become the weeper or the hater. But if you're in a vulnerable state, angry DNA might not be helpful.

Yet there is one emotion that doesn't go away, since all the blood in the world will not change that: my love for him.

It requires quite some preparation to let him see me as the one he used to know before I became lost, missing, and then dead. Then alive again. I bring color to my paleness with brushes, lipsticks, and wands—which I order online and which are charged to my credit card. I put on a lovely dress, keep my teeth clean, and my hair brushed. I shower with cold water and spray perfume behind my ears. All this for him, to be on his earth, to be in his warmth.

I went missing for almost a year before I resurfaced. So much happened during those months, things I could not speak of, and that I cannot speak of even today.

I invited the vampire Phillip into my sanctum—my bedroom,

where I felt safe and warm—and then it happened. He was a lovely figure that seemed to float in the air. Why I pulled open the window I will never understand. I was hypnotized. I thought I was in a dream. Though I was in a relationship with my dear Marcus at the time—as I am today, again—I kept inviting him in. It's what you do when you're hypnotized.

During my transformation, I began to grow cold and to feel claustrophobic in my own home. I did not fit in there. I got angry at Mom over little things, just simple questions about college or how I'm feeling. "You haven't eaten!" she would say. I began to lock my bedroom door, especially at night. She thought I had lost my mind. Then I was gone. I flew away in Phillip's arms. I was his consort.

When Phillip's undead life ended at the point of a stake, I returned to my little world. There were no cameras around, which showed my importance to the world, and the police closed the case about me after a little interview. I had to pretend I wasn't lost, pretend that I had simply gone to find myself. After giving Mom my phone number, I left. All this, of course, happened at night.

My poor mother, she still believes I'm alive. I brought joy back to her, at least. But I do it all for him, for Marcus. I no longer visit Mom, though she has asked me to. I could travel there without a plane ticket. But we have nothing to talk about, and I can't eat her food or stay over.

I still get phone calls with promotions. Sometimes, I get questions about who I will vote for in the next election. I always stay silent before I hang up. I still pay my bills, my cellphone line. I try to be as alive as I can. All for him.

Tomorrow, I pay rent. I deposit the money order into the landlord's office mailbox at night before I go to work. Yes, I work. It's a part-time at a gas station from eight to two. The owner thinks I go to school in the morning.

Mind you, I could drop the money in the morning, even under the sun, without danger, as long as I do it quickly. But the sun burns the dead like nothing else, as if to remind its place. The great light peels or blisters our skin, and there is no cream for that. The sun reminds us who we are. If you ever see a man in sunglasses in the afternoon, in a mask that covers most of his face, or who is dressed like a Muslim woman, he's probably a vampire. Even in the daytime, vampires remain prisoners of the dark.

I have a confession of love: I am on a bloodless diet. I haven't fed in three weeks. Real hunger hits a vampire every four weeks—starvation every seven or eight. I hate having to feed after my own little four-week window, but I have no choice—without blood, my somatic sensors weaken. I want to be the woman that Marcus wants in the bedroom, and also not a monster. I think four weeks is a balance, though I'm pretty hungry on the fourth. Prior to my diet, I would leave North Hollywood every couple of weeks after clocking out of work and head to the mountains. It's a good place to hunt. There is always someone out and about, far from prying eyes.

Now I do it every four weeks.

I don't always let my prey live, of course. There is a reason for it. It is essential—I've been told by noble beings—to keep the number of vampires low. Not only do they go after our prey but can be stupid and unmask all of us responsible undead—and then we'd have to kill the entire world. We do not want to do that. We'll run out of room and prey and have to feast on each other in the end. That might be a bit difficult, everyone being a vampire, and no one likes recycled blood, at least not more than once, unless it is the one from your lover. But my lover is not undead.

How to kill a vampire? You don't let him become one. You drink for three or five minutes, then apply the stake. The time of transformation depends on how much you drink. It takes a soul a few days to turn if you drink one or two liters—an hour or two if more. At first, the victim is confused, tired, always wanting to sleep. To turn someone into a lover, however, requires several days of romantic pain, and very little blood each time.

This is what the great vampire lord, Trevor Luccan, taught me—or illuminated for me—when I told him about Phillip and my own transformation.

Yes, I have a small coterie of undead friends. We respect each other and protect those whom we love, even those who still live under the sun, like my mom. I would destroy anyone who touches her. Trevor has taught me a lot. He's a wise vampire with a lot of lore.

I asked him once why I still loved. He said that ghosts don't lack feelings.

"You know when your grandpa comes like an angel to protect you?" he said. "It's because his spirit still loves. Vampires are the same. We still crave a natural life and a part of that is love—though at other times it is revenge. A vampire who was evil in life is evil in death. One who was good, like you, is only a survivalist, and there is a difference."

Trevor, grand elder of an exclusive circle of undead—who is always dressed like he owned Westminster and a couple of other palaces—would not even kill a flower. He prizes life and loves a few who are still alive.

He is the most brutal killer within our exclusive group, and yet enchanting and caring with those he honors, like his father and his sister. He is not brutal just to be brutal. He's not a monster in his soul, but a dear soul who does not like to leave messes around, who cleans after himself and who, if he likes someone enough to make her a companion, will share all the bounty of his beautiful romance with her. He has five dames in his romantic collection, all who love him as a husband and respect him as a king.

"Lovely Adelia, look! The moon is like the sun tonight," Trevor says as I come into his little palace of a home in Pasadena on my night off. He is a tall, stalwart man. He is always sitting elegantly on the couch, legs crossed, a book on his lap, near a fire that does not touch him.

The women always look at me with wonder, yet quietly, with a look askance, a small trace of jealousy in their perfect faces, even as Trevor and I discuss Marcus, the love of my present and my past. As always, I nod to them, expecting no response, and they vanish into the walls.

Tonight, Trevor looks at my face with as much curiosity as his undead lovers. I feel as if I ought to touch my cheek to find what he has spotted, but I don't. Neither do I say anything.

"You look troubled," he goes on to say.

"Troubled, burdened," I reply.

"With love," he says.

"With hopelessness because of that love."

"Well, I have good news. As promised, here it is: the ring of eternity. As long as he keeps it on, he need not die."

In awe that such a ring could exist, I feel my undead heartbeat—if that is what it is—more strongly than ever. Yet with my shock comes questions: will Marcus consent to wear it for the promise of eternal life?

Before my death, I would have never consented to living forever, but now, with the opportunity to live dreams that an ephemeral life does not allow, I've come to see the advantages, even if I can never see the sun face to face again.

I used to think I was strange until I met Trevor. He held my hand when my memory was in a muddy place, my mind confused, and my soul in pain. A friend in death is a jewel in the undead world. Now he wants to help me keep the fire that once burned in my heart alive.

"We still won't be the same," I reply after considering many things. "One day, he'll find out—as he must. My truth will be impossible to hide, and he'll be terrified."

"Do you really think he would be? If you told him tonight you're dead—or undead—and became a spirit before his eyes—do you think he'd be scared? He might think it's a trick and keep believing what he believes."

"Eventually, he'll believe what I say and stop believing what he believes."

"Then I'll put away this ring, since it will bring you such pain."

"No!" I exclaim, fast at his hand with mine. Though I'm confused, there is no other way to attain my ends, unless I do what I fear, what I quail against. For I consider I still have honor, and will not steal a fruit but ask for it to be given so that I know it is truly mine.

"One condition," Trevor says. "Though you hold the ring, he must come to us for the ceremony. He must promise his eternal love for you and mean it. The ring knows if it is true or not. No ritual is necessary—no transformation—just his words and a true heart."

"I will bring him here," I say.

His lovers reappear after a little while. They have been feasting. Their faces look as if they muzzled their way into their prey. After such a feast, they're lusty. Trevor's shirt buttons jump off their eyelets almost in an instant. Passionate palms stroke his hairy chest, fangs and lips graze the back and front of his strong neck, and fingers make a mess of his perfect hair. Trevor asks if I would like to join. I decline the invitation and leave him alone to his sextet affair.

I leave with the ring. I carry it among the clouds, a faster way even for a spirit. Someone sees me opening my door.

"It's the first time I see someone entering that door." He looks like a neighbor, one I'd never seen. His round eyeballs protrude and look down at me and my short skirt even as he smiles. "You new here?" His black skin shines with some perspiration, as if he's been jogging.

I'm used to seeing humans and not attacking them after I am fed. Hungry, as I am now, the streets are my supermarket—their meat section—and I love shopping the most delicious meat. Yet he is not someone I would attack even if I had no choice.

As to his question, I don't know how to answer. I don't talk to strangers. I give him a look he sees as strange. His own words describe it.

"You must be from Northern Europe," he says. "They seem to look at people weird over there."

I still don't talk but give him the look of someone from Northern Europe. What that means, I don't know, but I turn and enter the door without saying a word. If only he knew I just saved his life, saved it from me!

"Bitch," he says as I close the door. "Fucking racist! Racists live in this building!"

I've heard worse. Yet it's not only the preservation of *him* that drives me away, but mine as well. Become friends with neighbors and they'll knock on your door. I try to leave neighbors alone.

I go to bed in the wooden box that I have furnished nicely like a coffin, though it is simply a long, rectangular box. It is in the long, dark walk-in closet. I am unconscious when the sun breaks.

3

Working

I talk, of course, at the gas station, but say as little as I can. Men, and even some women, tend to have a particular interest in me. I get phone numbers. Flowers. I've learned to ignore them all. If they persist for a few weeks—longer than it is safe—I make them my meal, and then I am at peace until the next Don Juan or Doña Juana comes along.

I feed early the next night before my shift, since it is now the fourth week. The blood will nourish my spirit a couple of weeks or so—despite stories, responsible vampires don't hunt every night. I had no choice, and I hated it for a moment. At least my customers are safe today.

To be honest—despite the diet I've forced upon myself—I think little of what I did, and feel more comfortable looking at people coming in and out of the store. I expect the next day there will be news of a "horrendous death" near a trail, but no one will know it was me. No one could commit a murder forty miles away and travel back in five minutes. And if investigators *did* realize I committed the crime—which to me was no crime—it would be difficult to put me in handcuffs.

"Forty on six," says a man in a baseball cap. Another puts a Monster and a pack of cigarettes on the tray under the bulletproof glass.

"You have to scan it," I say. The scanner is outside the glass. It doesn't take the man long to know what I mean.

A man in a suit asks me if I live in town.

"Yes," I say as I give him the change.

"You do the graveyard shift?" he asks as he puts his change into his pocket.

"Yes," I say, looking at him with my hands behind me. He's talking too much and I don't like that. Unless you're my human boyfriend or an undead friend, I don't like talkers. I can't tell the reason why, except that I'm a good soul, and would never pierce the neck of prey I'm fond of. In simple English, I do not become friends with my meal.

"You are the whitest chick I've ever seen," he says.

I keep staring at him and nod.

He makes a face understanding that I don't want to talk, raising his eyebrows, likely wondering what the matter is with "this chick!"

"You have a wonderful day," he says and turns.

Despite the bulletproof glass, I hear him outside, saying, "That broad is a bitch!"

I laugh.

It's true you become an animal when your rebirth is in darkness. A wild animal. Yet one more intelligent than the lion or the dolphin. Quicker than a mongoose. Keener of sight than the eagle. Wiser, even, than Plato and Confucius, for to us it is about death and life, and such are determined by strength, speed, and sagacity.

We do not care about atoms. They will not save us or feed us. All we care about is respect and passion. Both go hand in hand in creating a peaceful world, even among immortals, and in letting us experience feelings lost in death by willfully making a neck our drinking straw. We siphon our vitality from beating veins and are bent on using and not wasting it. Death is a terrible thing to waste, for in it you can do as you please, and never die again.

Unless...stakes.

Stakes are our foe, but they cause almost no headache. Vampires little care to carry them unless they make a mistake, in which case they go look for one to correct it. And humans little know we exist or that such instruments are needed for anything but to hold a camping tent.

Within my undead yet honest feelings exists Marcus, the quivering candle in the sepulcher of my body, the light in my darkness. Why my love for him didn't cease requires an explanation. The simplest answer is "I don't know." When I was with Phillip, even as I loved him as a companion, I dug deep into the sunless well of my memory. Phillip was a nice monster overall, but he could not compete with the jewel I had dredged from the dark waters, or with my past.

I suffered terribly, even as he fed me. The blood could not fill me the way he thought it would, the way it *should* have, being who I was. The emptiness he had left in me after turning me—the emptiness that only death causes on a spirit—cried out to be filled. I could not accept I had lost it all, even though my blood-love—which Phillip was with his looks and immortality—seemed to care much for me. There was love in me, beating in me, love for a past that had left me, even as my blood hunger deepened.

I might still be with Phillip today, but he had a fight with a vampire, a monster armed with a stake, and that was the end. If vampires can feel depression for being alone, then I was a good example of that. I had the pain of death in me. The loss that I suffered even in it when Phillip was no more. The other vampire never claimed me, as some would do of their conquered enemy's consorts. But I would have been an unwilling booty, and a feisty one, especially because I had been dying to resurrect and live again. Life had not left me, even in death. I desired the warmth I used to know, which I remembered well and missed. Even as I killed, I loved. And this hasn't changed. Yet I love more, now—more than when I was alive—because, though I could not die, I can count the years of Marcus's life as if they were only days, and I must cherish the brief moment.

Unless he slips on his finger the ring of eternity.

My four co-workers and my boss are the only humans outside my boyfriend that I am on speaking terms with—yet one has made me angry today.

Carlos, my replacement at two in the morning, is so late I could kill him. The clock ticks on the wall: 2:05, 2:10, 2:45! By the time he arrives, I'm about to strike. My fangs are out of themselves like flick knives when he says hi. My quick hand claps my mouth and I turn to my trench coat hung on the wall. Without saying anything—not even going over the tally with him—I leave.

I've had plans all day to see Marcus before dawn catches me—or gets so near my tail that my spirit's rear catches fire. It would be an unpleasant flight back home. I know I might get in trouble for leaving like that, but I'm so furious I don't care. I guess I would leave the owner alive after he gave me the boot, just so no one could imperil my happiness with Marcus.

Marcus is sleeping when I arrive. I knock on his window like a proper vampire, wishing for a mist to rise up around me to complete the image, but it is a clear night. I can see I'm half-vanished, nevertheless, since I am just appearing from the bowels of the air and the moon has been going through me. By the time he hears the knock, I'm completely visible.

It's not the first time I come like this. In fact, Marcus expects it, and he finds it funny and strange. I tell him it's the only way I can see him sleep when I'm not with him. I confess to him that I've often looked through the curtains simply to watch him, contemplate him. Every time, he doesn't know whether to call it creepy or romantic. He has called it both to my face.

But I indeed love to see him. I take in the sight and my breathless sigh leaves my emptiness, for I find him so beautiful. If I could, I'd surprise him with my arms around him as he slept. My cold skin would wake him, but afterwards he'd warm me with his touch, just enough to make me feel a little human again.

He doesn't open the window—of course not, he's a gentleman!—but leaves his room to get the door. When I'm inside, I kiss him, madly. He can feel my strength, his inability to escape me, even as he tries to reassert his manliness and his power over Woman. I let him have it—let him think I am weaker, and that he must protect me. In order for him to love me, he must feel like a man, the strong one. I have learned the script. It's the only way he can love me.

"Let's go to bed," I say. "I just came here to sleep with you."

"Is everything okay at home?" he asks, touching my cold cheek, pecking my cold lips, holding my cold hand.

"Yes, my apartment is a coffin."

He laughs and looks at me. I'm wearing a short skirt and he admires me. He's the only one I'm willing to delight in this way. His eyes raise my temperature in a positive way and warms my insides.

"Been out?" he asks.

"No. I just left work and came to you," I reply.

He grabs my waist and turns me about to see everything of me. I laugh and kiss him.

"Well, I guess it's decided that I must get up more tired than I thought," he says, laughing. He holds me. I love him. I am so alive with him. I forget so much about myself for the moment.

He turns off the lights and guides me into the bedroom. He holds me in the sheets, loves my lips and my neck, my nipples. Between my thighs, my blood-awakened chrysalis turns me into a happy butterfly. It's the blood I had before my shift that has made me so sensitive.

Oh, blood! I could not live without you! You give me wings and passion! If only I didn't need you to wake up my body!

I rise an hour before the sun gets up. I leave his body, his warmth, like a mist, and vanish into the night. I ache that I cannot see the sun with him, that I cannot feel its fingers on mine as they clasp to his. This is the pain of death. The dead always remember their sepulcher.

4

Some Company

It is difficult to think of a way to convince Marcus to wear the ring—or even utter the words to introduce it or explain what it is, or show it to him or confess that I have such a thing.

It's not that he'd gain "eternity" before the ceremony with Trevor, or that the ring is fail-proof, anyway. It doesn't stick to the skin, and it can be removed. The heart suffers no spell—a*live forever* doesn't mean *Love forever*.

But what else do I have? I do not want to give my love my curse. He wouldn't be the same Marcus. Even if he was— though separations are rare in the vampire world—who says that we couldn't separate? So, nothing is promised. Words cannot promise. Not even innate honor can promise its faithfulness. We are as bound to ourselves as to circumstances, like a bug is during the rainy season.

Aware of my incapacity in this matter, I went back to Trevor after work the next day, and asked him to do his magic during the ceremony, to convince Marcus to wear it. Trevor had to console my apprehension as if it were a head that needed patting, reiterating that he'll be honored to be part of an act that would bind Marcus eternally to me.

I now have set up a date with Marcus so we can do this, and so he can meet my friends—my friends in death, my support. He agrees to come with me to Trevor's little dark mansion on the hill.

The date is for Friday, six days from today. I show up to his house, as usual, around two. The time allows me to kill two birds with one stone: it lets me see him and see him alone. This time, I shudder—he has two friends with him. So there it is: I can't disappear. They can positively see my shock when I see them—my eyes must have gone really round.

"Adelia, long time no see!" says a very happy blonde. She hugs me and kisses me on the cheek. She's very happy to see me. "How are you? Where you been?"

If this was my house and we were alone, she would be carcass or slave—I let no one touch me who is not my boyfriend!

Yet, as she moves away, I finally recognize her. I feign a little joy.

"Melissa! It is wonderful to see you!"

"My god! You haven't changed one single teeny weeny bit!" she says with exaggeration. "You look like you haven't aged a single day! Doesn't she, Jer?"

"My god, Adelia, you look wonderful," says this Jer, standing next to Marcus.

"You don't remember Jeremy?" surprised Melissa says. "My boyfriend Jeremy? Well, ex-boyfriend." She raises her hand and shows me her ring. She's evidently very proud of it.

"Oh, congratulations," I say.

"Come here, baby," Marcus says, kissing the top of my head, then looking at his friends. "We usually spend the evenings alone." He looks at me again. "Sorry, forgot to tell you Jeremy was in town."

"Oh, it's okay." I get closer to him and lean my head on his chest. "Good to have you back, Jeremy," I say to the stranger I'm supposed to know.

"Thank you," Jeremy says. "How you been?"

"Perfect," I say. I'm struggling here—how does one act normal with strangers? My ol' bubbly me is dead! Yet I have to pretend. "Perfect" is the one word—simple and cold—that I can wrest from my bowels. At least I add a little smile. In spite of it, it seems to strike Jeremy as too cold a reply. He lowers his eyes with a puzzled smile.

"Good, good," he says.

Marcus tries to lighten the mood, which my discomfort has evidently caused. "How about we go to the kitchen for another beer?" he says. "Want one?" he asks me.

"Sure," I say, thinking, "Great, I have to stand this!"

It's not like I haven't spent time with people outside my dead circle. Even some of my old friends sometimes show up. They always come to Marcus's house—since they don't know where I live—and sometimes to my workplace. But the occasions are so far in between that I haven't been able to hone—or care to—the necessary skills to be warmer and more at ease. On the upside, my friends—if I can call them that now—have stopped asking me to "hang out" with them. They seem to notice my distance, my change. They are also safe from me, since I have good memories of them. I always wish to be the old me again, to hug and kiss people once part of my life without feeling the odd energy I feel now.

We go into the kitchen. It has a nice bar. I helped Marcus build it two years ago. I took two weeks off for that, getting myself into debt so I could pay my rent. Every evening around seven, I would be at Marcus's door with my own tools and other things he needed, and pretend that some things were "heavy" for me. Even now, Marcus lifts me up over his shoulder so that I can reach a glass in the top cupboard shelf—which I could get to by just levitating over the floor.

The bar has a base of wood, and we worked long hours—and many days—putting it together. I helped with the sanding, building the chairs—which we also did from scratch—and essentially redesigning the entire kitchen. I often would sprinkle water on my face to pretend I was sweating. The heater worked to my advantage. It warmed my materialized body enough that Marcus didn't wonder that it was still a little cold. We might have finished the job in a week, but we were always playing around, coming up with new ideas, and having a lot of intimate fun during breaks. The sex sometimes lasted longer than the work we put in. These were some of the happiest days of my undead life—and would have been even if I wasn't dead then. The joy I felt even managed to warm me up to people in general—at least more than now—though I was still a little distant.

We get our beers. Marcus sits next to me.

"So we're moving to Europe," says Melissa, continuing a conversation they were having before my arrival.

"That's awesome," says Marcus. "Where in Europe?"

"Estonia," Melissa replies.

"Estonia!" Marcus sounds surprised.

"Yeah, that's where my job is," Jeremy points out.

"Oh, right, you're in international law."

"Yup," Jeremy answers. "Will be working with the ambassador."

"That's solid. That's a great gig."

"A dream job," says Jeremy. "When are you going to graduate?"

"I'm just finishing my doctorate. A few months. I took a full two years from school, you know."

"You should have been done by now," Melissa says.

"Yeah, well, you know," Marcus replies.

Jeremy turns to me. "How about you, Adelia? When I met you, you were going to school too."

I can't believe he addressed me. Either way, I have to answer. I summon as much warmth as I can.

"Yes, that was a while ago."

"What was your degree?"

"Oh, I don't know," I reply. "It was not... I really didn't know what I wanted to do."

"You mean you didn't finish?" Melissa asks.

"No, not...not yet."

"You planning to go back?" Jeremy asks now. He smiles warmly.

"Perhaps. Eventually," I reply.

"Where you work at now?" Melissa asks. "You work?"

She's not impolite, but curious. All the same, I feel the weight of what I lost when I died—my education being one of them.

"Yes, at...at a gas station," I say.

"A gas station?" Melissa sounds surprised, then she smiles. "Well, that's work."

"All work is honorable," Jeremy says.

Melissa, perhaps feeling my discomfort, does something that someone else would have her hand torn off over—she reaches for my jacket.

"That's a lovely jacket," she says. "It's so soft. Feels like cashmere."

"It...it is," I say.

"Oh, my god, you must have shelled out a fortune!" she exclaims. "Look, darling, its cashmere," she says to Jeremy, still touching the fabric. "I need to get me one. *You* need to get me one!" She laughs now. "I hear Estonia is cold."

Jeremy laughs. "Where did you get that," he asks me.

"Here at the mall...Which one is it?" I ask Marcus.

"Beverly Center," he says. "We got it together. Ralph Lauren."

"How much did you pay for it?" the inquisitive girl asks.

I actually forgot. I look at Marcus to see if he can provide a response.

"You forgot?" he says, laughing.

I nod.

"It was almost three hundred dollars," he says. "I remember."

"Your face looks so stunning, too," Melissa says. "Last time I saw you, you looked almost the same. What do you do to your face—or is it just genes?"

"Just genes," Marcus replies in my stead. Then he looks at me. "I've never seen you do anything to your face."

"I never have," I reply.

"I wish I could look young forever," Melissa says. "You must exercise a lot, Adelia."

"A little," I reply.

"It shows," Jeremy says.

"Say, we were talking—me and Jeremy—about what it would be like to live forever, and look always young. Jeremy says it would be depressing. But if I looked like you, I'd be happy."

"Thank you," I reply. It may be the last thank-you the world ever hears from me—unless, of course, you're Marcus.

Either way, the talk of eternity surprises me—I'm even taken aback by it. It is obvious they don't know who I am—neither, of course, does Marcus—or they wouldn't be so nonchalant with the topic. I sip my beer, staring at the ceiling.

The conversation shifts to other topics that don't involve me. Jeremy and Marcus talk about past adventures together. All that time, Melissa, stares at me, perhaps wondering that I'm so quiet as I recline my head on Marcus's shoulder. She smiles as Marcus wraps his arm around me and strokes my head. At some point, she says, "You guys look so adorable together!"

Marcus laughs a warm laugh. "Thank you," he says. Then he kisses the top of my head.

"Marcus says you always come around at this time," Melissa says, addressing me.

"Yes," I reply.

"You do something in the daytime?"

"No, we just meet at night," Marcus says.

"Why's that?" Jeremy asks.

"Work," I say.

"You work the night shift?" Melissa asks.

I simply nod.

"Oh, wow, that must be tough."

"I want her to change her job," Marcus says. "But she seems to like it."

"I do," I say to him. "It's less chaotic."

"Why, you don't like people?" Jeremy asks, laughing.

I shrug my shoulders and sigh.

"That answers your question," says Melissa, addressing Jeremy.

It's a little past three in the morning when they leave and I'm alone with Marcus. I still feel Melissa's arms—which she threw around me before she left—all over me. I embrace Marcus as if to erase her essence. But I have a question as we go into his bedroom.

"Did you do something tonight?"

"We met for a few drinks," he says, simply. "Jeremy was in town and invited me. We just went to a bar that's close-by. Sorry, I should have called you. But I figured you were still at work. I knew you were coming by anyway."

"Yeah," I say. "I understand. It was nice of him to stop by."

"Yeah, it was."

"Maybe we can go out next weekend," I say.

"Sure," he replies.

Our clothes are off in a few minutes. We climb into bed together. His arms and the soft blanket warm me a little. I like feeling the rise of temperature on my skin—it makes me feel a little alive. Despite saying he is tired, a few minutes later he starts touching me and kissing my body. He goes under the blanket and kisses down slowly until he's thrilling me. It's a dangerous sensation—not for him, but for me. My fangs come out by themselves and, as he hides under the blanket, they are even more pronounced from the ecstasy. I regain control of them just in time before he can see me and kiss me. Half an hour after I service him, he's asleep. I can see the clock in the sky through the window. I put my clothes back on and vanish through the walls before dawn.

5

Movie Night

Leaving as I do always makes me sad. It also troubles me—Marcus always gets angry. And I understand. But how can I tell him the truth—that he's with a woman who no longer exists? A figment of his imagination who appears in human form, a memory who wants to be with him? Adelia is gone. Her essence is animated within a flesh that is no longer hers—a flesh that, to keep its motion, needs the thing that kept her alive before the grave opened.

Of course, I receive a few phone calls from him. It is nearly seven when I finally pick up.

"You just left again," he says.

I close my eyes in frustration. I hate these conversations. It's this love, indeed, that keeps me human, for I still have the emotions I would have had before my parting. Yet it's only with him that I am human this way.

"I know. Listen sweetie, I hate doing this to you, okay? I just feel that...I just want you to wake up and not have to tend to me while you get ready for the day."

"It's Sunday," he says. "I would have loved waking up with you. We haven't done that in a while. In years, actually. I don't understand why."

"It's..."

"I know," he cuts me off. "It's your job. I hate your job."

"I know you do."

"The woman I love is in a job I hate."

I sigh. "I know."

"Look, it's okay. It's late now. I guess you're going to work soon."

"Yes," I say. A lie—I don't work Sundays, but he has to believe I do. However, it gives me the opportunity for another lie. "But...I can take the day off, if you want me to. I know not much is going on, but we could catch a movie or something."

He's silent, as if reflecting. Then he says, "Actually, I have to work on my dissertation. But I'd love it if you came by. We can have dinner at home."

Dinner, yet again—what I do for love!

"What are we having today?" I ask.

"I don't know..." He pauses. "You like your steak bloody, almost raw. We can have that or...I don't know..."

"Yes, that sounds great," I say.

"Are you sure they'll let you take the day off?"

"Yes, I'm sure. I...I have a good record. I've been there a while. I've never stolen anything or killed any customer."

Here Marcus laughs. If he only knew my joke is not a joke—though I say it as a joke—and, in a way, mean it as a joke.

After we hang up, I go to the shower. Today, I turn on the hot water and wash my hair with an Herbal Essences shampoo—one with Jojoba Extracts—and rub a rose-scented Victoria's Secret bodywash all over me. I go into my closet, where my box-bed is, and extract a gorgeous dark-blue T Tahari midi-dress—it has long sleeves and a delightful white collar that blends with the white placket. It's longer than what I usually wear, the hemline falling to my knees, but I've been wanting to wear it for a while. I complement it with a navy blue beret and an old Hermès Paris watch—a three-thousand-dollar piece I paid with my University student loans almost six years ago, and one of the things I got from home before I left forever. Then, makeup. It takes me more than an hour to get ready.

So I "take the day off." I'm at Marcus's by nine—a good time considering everything I did to get ready. I park my 2017 Toyota 4Runner behind his car. Though I usually fly, there's something I love about driving—it makes me look and feel alive—who expects a vampire behind a steering wheel?

Marcus is outside on the porch when I arrive. I wave at him through the windshield before I step out. When I step onto the porch, his eyebrows go up, immediately.

"My goodness! We're just watching a movie on TV and vegging out," he says, laughing and kissing me.

"You know I always want to be ready just in case we go out," I say. "How was your dissertation?"

"Still going," he says. He lifts me up and puts me in his arms. "You look delicious. I want to eat you and your hat!"

"Before dinner?" I laugh.

"Fuck dinner! I rather have my dessert."

He bites my neck, softly, and kisses it. His lips go to mine.

I'm so happy he forgot this morning.

He carries me in. This is what I live for—what I thirst! Today, it will be almost four weeks since I went hunting—four weeks since anyone has disappeared on account of me. Whose DNA still courses through my veins, I don't know, but when I see the steak on the table—covered with aluminum paper—I almost get hungry for it—though I know it's just the expectation of the little blood I will consume—animal, though it be—that raises my craving.

Of course, he puts vegetables on my plate and a piece of bread next to the steak. On the plus, he brings out a bottle of wine instead of beer for a change. This I also crave—I'm an alcoholic—if I was human, I would have died at the hospital a long time ago—there are advantages to being a vampire. Of course, I binge only when alone, and never before work or before visiting Marcus—I'm a measured alcoholic.

I taste the veggies and the bread. Blah! They do nothing for me! I detest them! But I put on a show, and the steak is like a chaser of the baser things, though I wish its blood were different.

After dinner, we cuddle on the couch and watch *30 Days of Night*. I pretend to be afraid of some scenes—I hate seeing myself—and at some point, I get up, saying, "I can't watch that." I stand, looking away from the TV behind the couch.

"Oh, baby, I'm sorry," he says.

"Please change that movie," I say. "Or I will go. I can't be here."

I can hear his silence. I can tell he's surprised, even shocked.

"I'm sorry sweetie." He turns off the TV. "What about Beverly Hills Cop?"

"Yes, that's better," I say, without turning around. "I need to use the bathroom." I exit the room.

It was not an excuse. I *do* go to the bathroom, to its privacy. I lock the door and sit in its darkness, the only light the moon that comes through the window to see my tears. With so little blood circulating in my veins, they pour thin and watery, almost substance-less. I touch them. They feel like real tears. I get up and turn on the light quickly. I look in the mirror. Their tinge is almost plasmatic. But I need the darkness—the darkness that I'm trying to escape—to be now my shelter. I turn the light off and sit in the corner. I try to gain strength. To be happy again.

Oscar Wilde was wrong. We don't kill the thing we love—not unless you're a vampire! We are the only criminals. To kill love with a false word, a false kiss is not the same as killing life—literally taking it—with fangs! The ultimate sacrifice is someone else's death, not ours. We kill so that a shell, animated with someone else's blood, will wrap its arms around us! The spirit—the thing we love—cannot enjoy the world and the drinks and the passion of the flesh. That is why we try to keep it within something tangible—something of which members can sense and taste.

Marcus knocks on my door almost ten minutes later—I suppose it is a decent amount of time to get worried.

"Baby, are you okay?" he asks.

I turn on the faucet. "Yes baby! I'll be right out. I just felt a little... sick, that's all."

"Oh, okay. Are you okay now?"

"Yes, darling. I'll be right out."

I pour water on my face and wipe it with the used towel on the rack. Then I bring out my lipstick, my mascara, and my rouge. It takes me almost ten minutes to reapply the makeup. Quick though I am flying, this still takes time. Speedy application is a skill, and I'm jealous of teenagers who have mastered the art.

When I step back outside, I'm refreshed. I needed that time to come to some level of comfort. When we sit again, I think we're going to watch Beverly Hills Cop, but he has switched the movies. Instead, we watch *How to Lose a Guy in 10 Days*, one of my favorite romantic comedies.

However, once we start watching, I get depressed again. There is too much daylight in the movie. While we have watched many movies with suns in the offing, my feelings today cannot take it. Both day and night are my enemies at this moment. I turn to Marcus and ask him if we could play a game instead.

He touches my chin, asking, "Is everything okay?"

"Yes. I just don't feel like watching movies today. I just wanna spend time with you."

He turns off the TV with a smile, holds me, and kisses me. Then he touches my face. “Okay,” he says, getting up, taking my hand.

I get up as well. We go to the table and play Scrabble. When the clock strikes two, I leave.

6

A Day at the Job

I've said before that, outside of Marcus, the only humans I'm on speaking terms with are my co-workers. It's another act, though I find more commonality with them through the job. Sometimes, the till is short, and we go over the numbers. Sometimes, they tell me about the mean customers or their lives—or when someone stole something. Today, however—to practice more at this "social thing" –I spend some time with Carlos—the young cashier who made my fangs come out in anger when he came late to relieve me—outside in the back of the store where he smokes his cigarettes.

"Dog, you look pretty tonight!" he says.

"Dog?" I say.

"It's a compliment. I call you dog as a compliment."

We're sitting on the little sidewalk around the store, close to the customers' toilet.

"Ever gotten a girl naked after calling her dog?" I ask.

"Plenty of times," he says, dragging on his cigarette and letting out a large curtain of smoke. "Some of them don't care."

"Very interesting humans," I say, thinking like an undead, which I quickly consider a mistake. Carlos, however, seems to take it as regular talk.

"Yeah, interesting humans," he repeats. "They're not smart like us vampires."

I look at him. "Vampires? Are you a vampire?"

"All I need is my fangs," he says.

So, he's joking. But he continues, "We're vampires cus we sleep in the day and work at night."

"Is that what your life is like?" I ask.

"Except on the weekends. My clock resets."

"That's the difference between us. My clock never resets."

Another mistake on my part; yet Carlos shrugs it off.

"Yeah, some people don't work the same after having this job. But I like it. I'm not a daylight kind of guy."

I look at him. Everything I've said that should have made me afraid of revealing something simply washes off him as if my life is no different from other humans. Catching this, I say, "I'm a vampire."

"Dog, I already knew that!" He laughs.

I am shocked. "You knew that!"

"Of course, what normal human would work in this shitty place at such crazy hours?"

I begin to understand. He doesn't think I'm a vampire in a real sense, but in a rhetorical sense. That makes me feel both good and bad. I wish I could have a friend who knew the truth and accepted me for who I am. But I think my darkness is just mine, and I must live with it on my own.

"Get off the vampire subject," I say.

"What's wrong with vampires?" he says, laughing. "By the way, did you hear about the guy last night?"

The way he switches topics is incredible. He seamlessly makes me forget about something that nearly made me get up and leave and piques my curiosity with something new. He may be an artist with women—he offends them and then makes them laugh. I remember some things of my past—his type is what me and my friends used call "a player."

"No," I say.

"No one told you? He came in and knocked down one of the shelves. He was crazy, screaming some shit I didn't understand. It hit the shelf on the other side like he was playing dominoes."

"Did the other shelf fall?" I ask.

"No," Carlos says. "But it hit it pretty hard."

"What happened next?"

"Next? I came out with my pistols and stood in front of him—"

"Your pistols!" I interrupt.

"Yeah, my guns"—he flexes his arms and I think he's going to kiss his bicep—"my threatening look. He started throwing some racial slurs, calling me Mexican. I was like, 'Fool, I'm Guatemalan!'"

For the first time, I laugh. It surprises even me. I can't remember the last time a human made me laugh.

"That's how it was," he says. "He just run off into the dark, back to the shelter."

"Back to the shelter?" I ask, curious.

"Yeah, back to the homeless shelter," he says. "He stunk the whole place. I had to spray it. Even used my cologne. People came in saying the store smelled good."

I laugh a little again. He goes silent for a moment while I stare at the floor. Many thoughts are in me—one of them, the realization that humans are not so bad after all. A thing I'd forgotten.

Then Carlos looks at his watch.

"Okay, time to go back to the grind to pay the bills," he says, getting up. "Coming?"

I look at his hand. He's trying to help me up. I take it and stand up. I say, "Thank you." I feel emotional enough to cry. As we go around the store, I stop him. "By the way, if you ever get a girlfriend, let me know, so I don't suck her blood."

He laughs. "Yeah, that's my job."

I laugh again and we keep walking.

After the conversation with Carlos, I start looking at people differently. An old man comes in. He asks for a pack of American Spirits, Turquoise. He pays me with a twenty-dollar bill. After giving him the change, he thanks me, turns to leave and then stops with a smile.

"You're very pretty," he says.

"Thank you," I say.

This is very usual, and don't normally engage. This time, however, I add a little smile to my "thank you."

"Bye, have a wonderful night," he says, waving.

The next customers simply scan their items and pay with their cards without making any connection. "Hello" and "Thank you" are their only words through it all. Some throw in, "How you doing?" but that's all.

Carlos is at the register next to mine. As I ring the next customer, someone says out loud from one of the isles, "No more of this chocolate?" I look up. A man is holding a bar of chocolate. Carlos leaves the counter. When my customer leaves, the man and Carlos are walking together to the counter. Carlos goes to the other side to ring him up.

The man says, "This is gonna have to do. My girl's on her period."

"They're the bosses when that happens," Carlos says.

The man laughs. "She's always asking for Hershey's. But, anyway."

"Will she like the Snickers?" Carlos asks.

"If she don't, what can I do. I can't drive all around town just to look for a bar of chocolate. This is like the middle of nowhere."

"Yeah, that's right," Carlos replies.

"Alright! Thanks, man! Have a wonderful night!"

He says goodbye and even waves at me.

The next customer makes my eyes go round. Marcus appears, suddenly. His silent laughter is warm. I wave and smile.

"Hi," I say.

He leans into the glass at the counter. "Excuse me," he says. "I heard there was a hot babe who worked here. I was wondering if you knew her. I come from a long way off just to find her. Do you know who she is?"

"Well, sir, if she ain't me she'll be lying somewhere in the road in no time," I joke back.

Marcus laughs. "Oh you're a dangerous creature," he says. "Hello baby."

"Hello," I say.

He blows a kiss at me.

"What are you doing here?" I ask.

"Told you, come from a long way off looking for my hot babe."

"Well, I hope you find her."

"I think you'll do—for tonight." He winks.

I laugh. We play these games often.

"No, I was at the school library doing some research for my dissertation and decided to drop by."

"Oh, shucks," I say. "My break is not for another two hours."

"Oh, it's okay baby. I just thought I'd drop by. I got you this."

He puts a flower on the counter under the glass.

"Oh, baby! Thank you!" I say.

"Just go," Carlos says. "Don't worry, it's slow. I'll cover for you."

I look at him, impressed.

"Thank you, Carlos," I say.

"No problem," he replies.

I go through the door the divides the counter section with the rest of the store and hug and kiss Marcus once we're outside. His car is in one of the parking spaces in front of the store and we go inside. He kisses me there again.

"You look lovely," he says.

"Thanks," I reply. "How was the library?"

"Dead, which was good. I took off my shoes and put my feet on the couch in front of me."

"I knew you were a law breaker."

"And you're a heartbreaker," he says. His mouth goes to my neck and his hand to my bare thighs.

"Oh, baby," I say.

"I need to warm up these cold legs," he says.

"Oh, god, baby, I wish you could! But then I'd have no job."

"Hey, that would be good," he continues, nibbling on my ear. "We can spend all day together."

"You're silly," I say, but I know what he's aiming at. I hope we don't have to talk about me having to quit again.

"I just need a little bit of you." He kisses my mouth. His hand is suddenly on my panties. "Hmm...I think this is warm," he says.

I'm glad he stepped off the subject. His last words make me laugh. "You're making it warm," I say.

It's likely he made me warm, since that is still a sensitive area. However, it's not as warm or sensitive as it would be if I had more blood in my system. He does a good job enough to bring me some thrill when one of his fingers digs in. I sigh. My hand goes instinctively to his lap and I bite my lip.

"Oh, baby, you're making me mad—mad in a good way." Then I look up. A man is walking in direction to the door of the store. I arrest Marcus's hand.

"Wait, people are going to see us," I say, laughing.

He throws himself back on his seat. "Oh come on!"

"Baby, this is the parking lot!" I say. "Unless you want to shoot a movie..."

"That would be awesome," he says. He raises and lowers his eyebrows comically.

I laugh.

"Are you coming home today?"

He calls his place "our home." It both hurts me and makes me happy. I take his naughty hand in mine and kiss his fingers. "Sure, why not."

"Good. Or, actually...wait, that will be late again. No. I know why you do it. I love having you, you know. But I'm sure it's a struggle.

That's why I don't like this job. Not just because of me, but because I know the sacrifice you make."

I touch his face, tenderly. He cares for me. I look deeply in his eyes and kiss him.

"I won't take it personally if you just rest for one day," he says.

"I know," I reply. "We'll see."

"Okay, go on to work, you heartbreaker! I'll see you later."

He kisses me again. When he leaves, I feel both happy and empty, a strange feeling. I'm happy because he came and because I got to spend time with him, but his leaving also took a part of me.

7

Taking Risks

The gas station is one of those out-of-the-way pitstops for people traveling cross-state or cross-county. It is isolated from other businesses, and the road to it is almost dark. At work we call it "The Shining Gas Station on the Hill," though the way to it is flat and straight. It is twenty miles from Marcus's place. It takes me thirty minutes by car from my apartment—I fly even when I'm in it. But it's not as quick as the scenic route through the clouds, which I sometimes take, telling people I was 'dropped off.

Marcus drops by now and then on his way to or from school, though not too often—which is why I'm always surprised and happy when I see him. A couple of times, he has taken me to the back of the store—which faces nothing but mountains—and made love to me standing up. He likes the open air—though sometimes we use the customers' bathroom, which is always locked and always "out of order," especially as we have bathrooms inside the store. One day, my revenant veins were full of blood from some passionate woman, which made the meeting more incandescent. After kissing me and touching me against the wall—his hand under my skirt, his mouth pulling down my top and biting my nipples—he unzipped his pants and bounced me against the wall with the motion of his hips. The back is a great place for intimacy—as long as people are working and not coming for a break. There are no lights there, so it is always dark at night—which is the only time I work. There are plans for a parking lot in the back, but right now there are only bushes and earth. You can barely see anything in the darkness, which—despite the illuminated front—is almost pitch black.

I spend the next few nights with him—always after work. On Thursday, however, before the day of the ceremony at the vampire court—which he is unaware of—I take another day off. It is a risk to do so, but I got someone to cover for me—a thing I hate doing, since that requires picking up the phone and talking to people. But I have a good reason for it. I want to surprise Marcus.

After checking the weather, I see that it'll be cloudy with a 50% chance of rain. I get ready as usual, then cover myself like a Muslim woman—meaning I wrap a scarf across my face, put on a large hat, pull gloves over my hands, throw a thick jacket on, and put on pair of sunglasses. I talked to him earlier and knew he'd be home.

I park behind his car again. This time, I don't go to the window but straight to the door. Before I ring the bell, I look around. With the sun in the clouds and me being all covered, I'm not burning, yet I wonder if it would be safe to remove the scarf, the hat, and the sunglasses. What would happen if I did? I'm afraid, but I close my eyes and sigh. I take them off, waiting to burst into flames, and ring the bell.

"Please, come quick!" I plead, softly. "Please!"

A few seconds later, the door opens. He is positively shocked.

"Darling!" he exclaims. He looks at his watch. "Five-thirty in the afternoon!"

"Can I come in?" I ask.

"What a question!" he laughs. "Come here."

He pulls me in by my gloved hand.

"What's with the gloves and the big jacket?" he asks as I quickly close the door.

"Oh, you know. Didn't know how cold the day would be."

"What's the occasion? You're here early. This hasn't happened in years!"

"Oh, please don't remind me. I miss you, constantly. I hate my job, too, but...I have to keep it."

"I see." He nods as if understanding and not understanding. "Well, let's not talk about it. This is quite a surprise. Want a beer?"

"That would be lovely," I say. "Or do you have anything stronger?"

"A celebration for you coming early?"

"That's a good reason—but any reason is a good reason for strong drinks."

He laughs. "Oh, you alcoholic!"

We go into the kitchen. He pulls down a bottle vodka from a shelf and pours it in two glasses. He mixes whiskey and orange juice with it, and drops some ice. It's our own, unrefined invention of a cocktail drink. We call it Love and Fire, just what I love. We cheer with our glasses and drink. Then we kiss. After the kiss—his mouth still close to mine—he tells me he needs to use the bathroom. I laugh. When he leaves, I go around the house and close all the curtains.

When he comes back, he notices his home is a little darker.

"Did you close the curtains?" he asks.

"Yes," I say. "We can light up a candle and make it more intimate."

"A candle..." He checks his watch. "At five-fifty in the afternoon? Or evening, whatever you wanna call it."

"Sure, why not," I say.

"Oh, let's have a candle dinner! We haven't done that in a while."

"That would be lovely," I say. "Will we have raw steak again?"

"All bloody for you darling. But I'll need to go to the store to get the meat."

I put my hand on his. "Oh, not yet. Let's wait till it gets a little darker. That way, we can both go."

"Why couldn't we go now?"

A mistake. I said the wrong thing. I think quickly. "Well, we...we could but...I...I just got here and I...want to spend some time with you."

"Got it. I understand. Hasn't the drink lit up a little flame?"

He comes close to me. He clasps my gloved hand. He looks at it. "I love the gloves but they're in the away. Let's get your hands naked and...you as well, shall we?"

We're soon in the bedroom. As we cuddle, I remind him about the next day and ask him if we're still going.

"Sure," he says. "I don't mind."

Overall, the day—which soon turns into night—is just as I had wished. Around two in the morning, with the excuse that I have to cover for someone at work, I leave.

The rain pours as I drive. What would take me five minutes by clouds—rain or shine, or moonshine—takes me almost forty minutes. There is a flood somewhere slowing traffic. As I stop along with all the other drivers, I look up. I see someone flying. Another vampire. He's moving slow, as if he's looking for something. I would not be surprised. It's the appropriate time for a hunt. The rain adds a new layer to the dark. As I see him go, I think of myself. That must be how look to other vampires—since people can barely see us and wouldn't know what we are if they did.

Tomorrow, I will have blood without needing to hunt. It's been more than four weeks since someone disappeared because of me. I will cherish the blood I get tomorrow. It will make my body far more sensitive—more passionate. Then I can rest at ease for another couple of weeks before hunger strikes and the diet continues.

8

The Court of Vampires

As we head there in his car—and I sit with my seatbelt on next to him—Marcus asks me why I can't come early more often, that the night thing is tiring him. He tells me I have changed so much since *a while back*. He doesn't bring back my disappearance or anything he thinks might bring bad memories.

As always, I tell him about my graveyard shift, that I must sleep in the daytime, and that my rent is really high, which is the reason I work every day—and that is partly true, though I only work six days a week.

But the conversation takes another turn. He stops the car and we have what is called a *spat*. I would not tolerate argument from anyone, but Marcus really has me in his clutch. I feel terror, panic, agony at the thought of losing him. I feel so utterly weak with him. It's another mystery I must discuss with Trevor.

"You know I love you," Marcus says.

I love to hear that and I smile. But he continues.

"This few hours a day and only at night thing when I'm about to sleep or I'm sleeping...I don't know how I feel about it sometimes."

Here I feel I must defend myself.

"You have to understand my life is not the same. I want to share so much with you. Why can't you understand that? And it's not like we never do anything."

"Yes, I know. But it's only at night. Yesterday was like a fluke, and I hate that feeling. I want to be with you in the daytime as well." He touches my face. I lean my cheek on his hand and kiss his palm.

"Listen, I understand. I don't want to pressure you. But you understand?"

"Yes, I do," I say. I look out the window.

"You have to change your shift."

"Okay," I say.

He goes on to tell me of things he'd like to do, like go to the movies, have a sundae. All in the daytime. I've had sundaes with him—horrible things for me—and gone to the movies and to clubs and bars, but it's been at night. He'd like to take me to lunch one of these days, he says.

"Yes, let's do that sometime," I say.

"Let's do it tomorrow," he says. "You can take the day off, or the night off. Call off tomorrow night so that you can sleep at little at night and be refreshed in the morning. That's two days off. You need them. I want to watch the sunset, or even the sunrise, with you."

"I can't," I say.

Suddenly, I feel there is more he wants to tell me. He gives me *the look*. The kind of look that comes during a breakup. There is disappointment and frustration in his face. All he says, however, is, "Okay."

"I already called in today so that we could do something together," I say. "That's two days in a row."

"So we can go meet your friends? You don't see your other friends anymore."

"I do sometimes, but I rather not talk to them."

"Oh, you just *see* them!" He laughs.

We arrive at Trevor's place. Trevor is dressed to the nines in an exquisite suit that perfectly matches his lord-of-the-night persona. Marcus is dressed casually in a button-down shirt, a pair of jeans, and nice shoes.

Trevor's eternal companions are also with him. They remain quiet as Trevor extends his hand to Marcus very pleasantly. There are other vampires in the house, all elegantly dressed, which means Trevor is holding court.

"What a pleasure to meet you," Trevor says. "Please, come into my little dark palace."

There are some lights in the house, strategically placed in corners so they don't bother the eyes.

"Beautiful place you got here," Marcus says, looking here and there.

"Us creatures of the night must do our best to enjoy the finest things in life to compensate for the lack of that beautiful sunlight you yourself enjoy."

I see Marcus pause in mid-laugh. He is surprised at Trevor's style of words. He replies with his own style of humor, laughing somewhat. "Got it! So you only operate at night!"

"Chained to the dark like a bat," Trevor says, laughing.

The women look at Marcus from head to foot the way one looks at a delightful piece of meat. I see them lick their lips with an interest that terrifies me, soft and quiet though it is.

Don't let him spend the night here, I think.

We meet the other vampires as we enter the parlor. There is an immediate reaction of surprise as they all get up from their chairs. There is a chorus of stares and sniffing noses. I know what they scent—sweat from living glands, a human.

Even with Trevor as a guard, I am not very comfortable. I feel like a knife, or a fang, is never too far away—even from a noble vampire, one ready to correct an offense. But I know most of the vampires, and that they would never disrespect Trevor's house or his guests. It is a code of honor among the noble society to which they all belong.

One of interest to me is Henry Tubald, who, for some reason, veers from me to Marcus and then back again, as if he suspects something. While elegant and handsome, and one desirous of my hand for eternity, my heart—or even just my hand—does not belong to him, though I respect him.

There are many small tables in the room. Four have playing cards, another a chessboard—for vampires don't like to spend idle lives—or deaths—and one has bottles of wine. A marble table stands against the wall full of flowers, while the small crystal teatable before the main couch has a number of golden goblets, emptied of the blood they recently contained. Around are other elegant pieces of furniture, contributing to the almost regal atmosphere.

"Welcome, welcome," Trevor says, walking in.

He goes directly to the goblets. He picks them all up and hands them to another vampire with a respectful bow, as he is not a servant.

The vampires still stare. Trevor looks at them all. "My friends, let me introduce you to a friend of this house, Marcus Fenwick!" Trevor knows the name. "And, of course, you know our Adelia. Marcus and

Adelia are together. Thus, he has a special status in our house. As they say in the world, they are boyfriend and girlfriend. But more than that, they are eternal companions."

They all seem shocked at this revelation.

"How is this possible?" asks one of the vampires. It is Henry Tubald, still looking at me, then at Marcus.

I can hear the ladies talk among themselves. "Boyfriend and girlfriend," they whisper.

Trevor tries to pacify what appears like a little tension. The vampires are obviously surprised. Some even look offended. It's as if Marcus constitutes a trespass into their sacred realm. "Marcus comes here to make our acquaintance, and, if possible, to join us in our eternity," Trevor says.

The vampires look at each other, then at Marcus, then at Trevor, then at me, then at each other again. Out of the blue, one of them starts to clap. The sound is almost immediately answered by another. Then everyone.

"Well, it is good to have you here, Marcus Fenwick!" says Richard Skipp, a young, one-hundred, thirty-year-old vampire. He is elegant and tall, and looks older and wiser than the age when he died. He approaches Marcus and puts a friendly hand on his shoulder.

"Well, thank you very much," Marcus says. "I didn't mean to cause an uproar."

"It's a welcome uproar," Richard says.

"Welcome to our circle," says Susan Fredsome. She's a nice vampire and knows a little of Marcus. She raises a glass only filled with wine.

In time, Marcus knows everyone. It is evident, however, that the surprise among the vampires hasn't ended, and that it is only respect —and, perhaps fear—of Trevor that reins in both their elevated and baser natures. Marcus is not used to this sort of attention. He says thank you many times. When he sits down on the couch, to which Trevor has invited him, he says, "Join you in eternity?"

"You'll learn in time what I mean." Trevor sits next to him. I am so happy for him in our world. I know Marcus would be safe with him, even if they were alone. "That is what we say here. We are all 'nighttime laborers,' if you must know, and are not good friends with the sunlight. It bothers our eyes."

"That is very interesting. But now I understand how you know Adelia. She's also a nighttime laborer."

"Indeed, we got acquainted on a night like this. But tell us something about yourself. I hear you're still in school"

"Yes, law school."

"A noble trade."

"Thank you."

"And is Adelia the only one in your world—or, being good-looking as you are, do your passions change from day to night?"

Marcus laughs. "What a way ask if I'm faithful! Seriously, even if I wanted to cheat, I don't have time."

"I see. You are occupied most of the day."

"Yes, work and law school keep me pretty busy."

I chime in here, sitting across from them. "So you see? I would be quite a distraction in the daytime."

Marcus smiles at me.

"You are going places in life. That is very good," Trevor says.

Marcus turns to him. "That is the goal."

"So you love Adelia well."

"Well, we've been together for almost four years. Or five if you count the year that...yes, I love her well, as you say."

Trevor smiles. "That is great to hear. And that is all you need. That, of course, and the desire—or the willingness—to spend the rest of your life with her."

Marcus frowns slightly at this strange statement—even one who loves deeply and wishes to be tied forever would, I think, frown at that.

"It's an intriguing question," Trevor says, acknowledging it. "But, if that were possible, would you spend eternity with her?"

"That's a very strange question," Marcus says. "Are we getting married today?"

Trevor smiles. "You might."

Marcus doesn't reply. He looks at the carpet instead. He notices a golden goblet that one of the vampires left on the floor. Trevor, in his haste, overlooked it. He corrects the mistake by picking it up and taking it away, not before asking,

"Would you like a drink?"

"I would love one. What do you have?"

"For you, we have wine."

"For me?" Marcus laughs.

Trevor laughs back and walks away.

Marcus turns to me, still laughing. "For me?"

I laugh with him without commenting.

Trevor returns with the wine and two glasses, and sits down. "This is a most exquisite one," he says, pouring the wine into his and Marcus's glasses.

"Now the wine is for you, too." Marcus laughs.

Trevor echoes the laugh. "Indeed, we drink wine here as well, but shun it when we have something better—or we put the fine wine in that something better, if you get my drift."

"What's that better thing?" Marcus asks, lifting his glass to his lips.

"Oh, curious cat!" Trevor laughs, lifting his own glass to his mouth. "That better thing is life!"

Marcus smiles and nods, mystified. He observes goblets on other tables. Marcus asks about their content. Trevor only says, "A life-giving nectar."

The scent of flowers abound, a vampire's favorite, which drowns any hint of what the goblets might contain. Marcus, seeming to sense a secret, challenges Trevor with a laugh uniquely masculine and teasing, to be a "brave creature of eternity" and show him what is in the goblets. Trevor likes the teasing. He laughs and tells Marcus that the contents are a secret.

"We hold the secret for a while as we find out more about you. Trust me, when you find out, it will be nothing to fret about. Call it a club secret. Once you are part of the club, you will laugh that you thought the contents so suspicious."

Magic. The lie works. It lowers Marcus's guard and puts him in a relaxed mood. He obviously can't wait to be entertained by the discovery of the goblets' content, and soon starts talking with Trevor about different things.

9

The Vow of Eternity

Trevor doesn't show his fangs, figuratively or physically, but Marcus already thinks—as it is obvious by his glances around the room, and despite his more relaxed disposition—that this is an odd crowd. All the same, he has partaken of wine and good conversation. Trevor has made it easy for him—and for me, too—to feel comfortable after the awkward reception and the knowledge that Marcus and I are together.

Of course, no one has shown a fang, and the women have largely kept their eyes to their company—except now and then when they turn them to my mortal man with obvious interest in his neck and his soul.

Susan—the lady of the immortal world I trust the most—and I have occupied an entire corner for ourselves. With all the chatter and laughter around us, it is plain that the sensitive vampire ears are occupied, since no one looks in our direction. But it wouldn't matter if they *could* hear us, since we are telling no secrets. All the same, I like it that we are keeping our own conversation private.

"Oh, don't get me wrong. I've been looking, too, but he is taken," she says. "You wouldn't blame a *vampiress* and all the other damsels of the night for having our interest piqued by such beautiful meat."

"I know I can trust you," I say to her. We are drinking goblets filled with blood—which I am happy for, since it helps ease the pain of my blood hunger, which I rarely quench now due to my diet. For now, Marcus is safe, and the male vampires can have a good conversation with him without ogling his neck, though I'm sure they look at it from time to time, since it is *right there*.

"But why do you think he'd want to join you in eternity in such a way? Would he even believe the ring has the power to give him eternal life?

"I have thought of that and don't know what to think."

"Why not just make him eternal the proper way?"

"No, I couldn't. I would feel like a murderer. I would kill the precious thing he is."

"You love the human in him."

"Yes," I reply.

As Susan watches me with a sigh, I turn to Trevor and Marcus to hear what they're saying now.

Trevor is patting Marcus's leg. "Lawyers are always welcome in our world."

"Your world or the world in general?" Marcus asks.

"How the world outside my little realm sees lawyers, I don't know. I hear they're vampires."

Marcus laughs. "You mean blood-suckers!"

"Exactly. Now, that's one thing I like about them. Though the blood they consume has a green color, one of my favorites."

"I hope to suck a lot of those greens myself one day," Marcus says.

Trevor laughs. He is an effective host. He takes as he gives in the game of banter, making the moment pleasant.

Inquisitive eyes still linger on Marcus. Some vampires are still in awe that he is with me—one of their kind—while the women still thirst for him.

It's obvious Marcus notices the discrepancy between Trevor's pleasant bubble and the way others seem to analyze him.

I talk to Susan a little longer. After a few minutes, we are interrupted by Trevor standing up and saying in a loud yet pleasant voice,

"The time has come to inaugurate our great immortality—about time, I must say, after so long living secretly and quietly—and to be able to share it, through a gift, with a worthy man. Marcus, come here."

Marcus gets up. Trevor puts his hands on his shoulders and welcomes him to "his world," then asks him to sit again. Marcus is confused at being "sent back," but does so. All the vampires gather around the sofa. Trevor looks at me now and extends his hand. I approach and take it. He smiles at me and then at Marcus.

"This is a special occasion," he says to him, then turns to me. "Go on, Adelia, sit down and hold your man's hand."

I do so. Marcus kisses my cheek when I sit down.

Trevor smiles at this and says, "As I thought, there is true love here."

Marcus is somewhat drunk from the wine but still rational. It is plain he thinks the whole scene funny and odd.

"Are you a minister?" he asks. "You *do* look as if you're going to marry us!"

"I'll do much more than that," Trevor replies. "See this thing over here? It is yours to keep and to live forever."

Marcus stares at the little ring box Trevor is holding. "As long as I'm happy, I don't mind living forever," he says, suddenly. But even as he laughs, he looks mystified. "Are you proposing to me?" he asks then, trying to be humorous.

"I am proposing to you to live an eternity in company with your beloved, and to be a faithful man till the end of time and the universe—since that will end us all."

Marcus throws himself back on the couch with laughter.

Trevor extends his hand with the ring. "This is your gift, the gift that a righteous soul and unwavering love is deserving of. This was forged in the fiery caverns of Mantheluse, a place where only the invited go. It exists within the fabric of space. Inside the air. Spirits appear from within and pull you in whenever you are deserving to go. Wearing this gives you a window into it, even if you're not part of it. All Mantheluse needs is that you be part of its eternity, however it comes. Only a car crash can kill you, or a train crash, etc. Anything that tears your body apart. But you can survive water—except its pressure if you go too deep, so don't go too deep. But you cannot drown, not while the ring is on your finger. Once it is, it will be like being married to your beloved, your beautiful Adelia, your best friend. She loves you well—much more, in fact, than any mortal or immortal can love."

Through this recitation, Marcus laughs. His eyes go positively round with shock and admiration.

"Okay, so if I wear this, I can eat raw steak and suffer no stomachache or death. That's what you're telling me, unless the steak becomes a semi."

"Exactly," Trevor says.

"And this 'Mantheluse' will be happy?"

Marcus still can't believe any of this—or, even yet, comprehend it. He seems fascinated by Trevor's talk of the 'spirit world' and thinks it's all a joke. So tethered is he to what he knows of the living world that he doesn't believe in anything outside of it.

"Then what are you waiting for, man? Give it to me." Marcus laughs, reaching for the ring box.

"I will, but first the vow," Trevor says.

"The vow?" Marcus is puzzled now, even his laughter not hiding his incredulity.

"Yes, you must promise to tell no one of what we are going to show you."

Here I am about to protest. It will do no good to show Marcus that we are all vampires. Even if he doesn't believe it, he'll think we're freaks and completely demented. Or he'll think that he's gone mad, believing that what he sees is not what he sees. If the latter, he might escape. If the former, he might excuse himself to talk on the phone and never come back.

Then we'd have to kill him.

"It is important," Trevor says, looking at me, seeing my reaction.

"What's going on?" Marcus asks. He looks as if he wants to get up but is unable to know what action to take. I don't blame him; my little clan has suddenly the look of an Al Capone court, though there is no violence.

"Raise your left hand," Trevor says, solemnly.

Marcus frowns a little—the "joke" is beginning to look weirder to him. "My left hand?"

"Yes, you vow to keep our secret a secret and to love Adelia very much till the end of the universe."

"I can swear to the second very easily, but the first..." Marcus looks at Trevor straight. He has become defensive. The laughter, the joke, seems to have vanished.

"You love Adelia and that should be enough for you to hold the secret, since she is a part of it. Swearing to keep our secret means swearing to keep Adelia safe, something which I'm sure you'd like to do."

"Safe from any monster that wants to hurt her, yes."

"Very well, raise your left hand."

"This is not necessary," I object. "Just swear, we will believe you. You don't need to raise your left hand."

Trevor looks at me. I know the danger is greater if Marcus doesn't raise his hand—but if he is to love me, and be safe, the vow without the revelation might be the safest road for us and for him. I don't know if Trevor can read my mind, but I aim to transmit the message through my eyes.

"I swear," Marcus says without raising his hand.

"We trust you," Trevor says, bowing slightly though with finality, an act that means he consents to my request, one which would save Marcus's life, and puts the ring, not in Marcus's hand—as he was supposed to—but in mine. He pats my shoulder with a warm look in his face and turns. He takes a golden goblet from a white stand and goes over to Richard Skipp, who is standing with his arms crossed. They start talking about unrelated issues.

I hug and kiss Marcus and hurry him out the door. Our time here is done. He puts on the ring that Trevor offered, especially since at the end it came from my own hand.

"If you'd like to test your eternal life, let me know," I say as we drive back. "We'll go swimming in the Atlantic, and swim all the way to Australia. You can do that now, you know?"

There are many things Marcus obviously wants to ask me. He gives me that *other* look—the confused, disbelieving, and even wondering look. His wondering is perhaps about the people I associate with. At the end, he echoes my suspicion.

"You got a weird group of friends 'yond that hill," is all he can summon to say.

"In time, you'll understand," I say, though so softly I think I only hear myself.

10

Grappling With Things

The next day, I am desperate. Did I make a mistake in bringing Marcus to Trevor? Something tells me things have changed. As a dutiful girlfriend, I show up to his house again after work all the same. I look at him through the window.

He's sitting on the bed with a book on his lap, bedroom light on. He can't see me as he reads. I'm also a ghost, my inner me—whatever it is that makes me—afraid to interrupt him, as if the interruption will reveal an unsavory secret—that he doesn't want to see me, even though he knew I was coming. I called him from the gas station, where I only worked for an hour—telling my boss, who luckily was there, that I wasn't feeling well—and indeed that was not a lie.

Thus, I'm early. It is only nine in the evening. As I look at Marcus, who is all pensive as he reads down a page of his book, I plan my next move. Yes, I think we should go out, forget yesterday. That will allow us to get back early and spend an intimate time together.

I caress the window as if it were his skin and close my eyes. I want to reach him without touching him, and still feel him as if I were touching him. It's an odd paradox, a contradiction that anyone in love can understand. But I must show myself, regardless of his feelings. Thus I tap on his window, becoming materialized before he can look up.

He sees me. I smile and wave. He puts his book down and goes out of the bedroom to the door.

One thing that is true in mythology is also true in my real life as a vampire. There is a cosmic rule that binds all of us immortals. We cannot come into a place without being invited. Could we break in? Throw a rock through a window so we can reach the latch and open it, or shatter the glass, completely? I have not tried. According to Trevor, we couldn't. Something stops us, something immaterial, yet harder than a thousand-mile-thick wall.

For those who fear vampires or monsters, this is a good rule of thumb: don't open the window.

When Marcus opens the door, I feign joy. He answers to my pretense with his own happy face. He stares at my short dress, which I wear because I know he likes "short things." Even a *vampiress* must please a man, know what he likes. Whatever he remembers of the night before seems to dissipate at sight of me, for I prepared myself very well.

He pulls me to him, not by my waist but my legs.

"You're cold."

"That's the thing about always coming at night. But I bring them for you to warm."

He kisses me. It's just a little peck, but I close my eyes. It brings me comfort. My desperation sinks under his reassuring touch.

"I was wondering if we should go out tonight," I say.

"Sure, what would you like to do?"

"Anything you want. It's my treat. I just got paid."

He laughs.

"You don't mind a woman paying for you, do you?"

"A stranger? Yeah. My girlfriend? Please, pay every time!"

I laugh. I feel so at ease now.

Correction. Not *too* at ease. In fact, I don't know what I feel. It is an *uneasy easiness*, a *cautious easiness*, even while much of my fear has gone away.

I notice one thing that pains me, however: he's not wearing the ring.

I don't know if I dare bring it up. But I suddenly have an idea—even as he takes my hand and takes me into the kitchen where he grabs two beers from the refrigerator, something he always does before we go out. I will buy a ring tomorrow, or make him buy me one, a cheap one, not an engagement ring. Maybe that will make him put on Eternity on his finger, and I can have him, forever.

He gives me a beer and offers me a piece of strawberry cheesecake.

I pretend to enjoy it, even though I can't feel its rich flavor or care much for it. My taste buds can only truly taste three things, blood, strong alcohol, and my man's juices.

I so much miss my normal life. I have barely grown old, while Marcus has developed into a thirty-year-old, mature man. He has often told me how I still look like when he first met me. I tell him I have *good genes*, and to look at my mother, who even at fifty-one still looks like she's forty. I am only two years younger than he is, and will look twenty-three until he's eighty, unless he wears the Ring of Eternity, which will keep him young forever, even if he never becomes undead.

I treat him to Five Guys, his favorite burger joint. I order my meat rare, almost bloody. Though animal blood doesn't do much for me, it is better than the meat. I have not gone on a hunt for almost three weeks. My only nourishment has come from half a goblet at Trevor's place during the ceremony. My taste buds can barely stand the meat, but it's a sacrifice I'm willing to make. It's a necessary sacrifice. I have tried to stop being a monster. All for love.

After the burger dinner, we drive to Quickies Bar. We stand in line to get in. I'm a little more voluble in these settings, though I don't do follow-up questions, I simply answer them. Mostly, I nod to people who address me. Some ask mundane questions such as, "Is this Wilshire?"

While standing, I hold on to Marcus as if he will save me from a fall, and hide my face in his chest. I'm a very tender girlfriend. He likes it that I ignore everyone, as if no one else existed but him.

Finally, we get to the bouncer. I show my ID Card. The bouncer tells me I look very young for the age I'm supposed to be, but lets me in.

Quickies is a nice, luxurious bar. I order a Vieux Carré, which they have on the menu. It is a strong drink, a mix of brandy and whiskey and other ingredients for flavor. Just what I need. The blood in my body reacts to it, its iron warms and makes me feel warm.

When I'm with Marcus, I smile at people more, which I would not do if alone. I thank and smile at the bartender, though I don't chit-chat with him. My smile is just like my order, totally transactional.

It's also a way to show Marcus the "warm side of me," not the uptight one when I am alone. It's only with him that I change. He doesn't like cold people, either toward himself or others. The amount of times I say "Thank you" is a condemnation I'm willing to put up with.

As we sit, I tell him—through the loud music—how I ignore men at the gas station. I tell him I even get phone numbers from old men. I confess to him I am very cold at the gas station, but also that I have to—so many people want to be my friends or "something else."

Marcus laughs. He finally brings up what I knew would come up eventually: the night before.

"What's with this ring of eternity?" he asks.

"Oh, I know," I say, almost dismissing it. "I don't know why he made it sound like... Trevor just wanted to see how you'd react to...to this tale of Mantheluse. He's just crazy."

It pains me to paint the noble Trevor in this light, but I have to ease Marcus and make him think it was all a charade to make him laugh.

"That was very interesting," Marcus says. "I thought he'd been drinking too much."

"No, he...he drinks but...barely. Or it doesn't really affect him." Suddenly, I come up with a lie. "No, I told him how much I love you. I bought the ring for you. It's just a promise ring. He said, 'bring him over for a vow.' I don't know why I was so silly to bring you there."

Marcus nods. "It's a weird crowd—though now that you tell me it was a joke...Maybe I was mistaken to think that. I thought they all had knives and were ready to butcher me. Like I interrupted an Al Capone meeting or something."

He wants me to laugh and I laugh in accordance.

A lie is such an important tool. A weapon. We need it both in the undead and the living world. A lie can sometimes tell the inner truth, even if it bothers us to lie sometimes. We will tell a dying grandma, who has lost her mind, that her husband will be coming soon, that he called and is on his way. That eases her. That gives her comfort. A lie is sometimes a weapon of love. And so I lie to Marcus, and so I accuse Trevor of being a jester, though a good-hearted one, and that the people in his house reacted weird for their own reason.

Marcus seems to buy it. It seems to ease him.

"Is it really that important to you that I wear that ring?"

I look up to him. "It would mean so much to me," I say.

He looks at me, a smile on his face and in his eyes. He kisses me.

My soul almost cries when he does. I throw myself in his arms, even though we're only sitting. I cannot cry, but he sees the shine in my eyes, a reaction of the alcohol.

11

The Danger of Brunettes

When Marcus gets up to go to the bathroom, I become myself again. I ignore people, even the bartender, whom I should be friendlier to. But I have a good excuse when he asks me if I'd like another drink—I'm sitting stiffly, looking up, aiming my eyes in the direction Marcus took, like a dog making sure he doesn't lose his master.

I seem to make an impression. A man asks me if I lost something. I ignore the voice. Don't even know who spoke. I keep looking ahead of me. The man loses interest when I don't respond. I must look quite odd to him, maybe to others as well. I sit like that for a few minutes, completely still, and then get up, abandoning the chairs that someone else might take.

I gravitate past the crowd without looking at anyone. It doesn't even feel like I'm walking. As I get to the hallway that leads to the bathrooms, I see him.

He's talking to a woman, a brunette with a dress even shorter than mine—her legs are like milk under the tight-woven red cloth it came out of. Everything about her is as pale as a vampire and as alive as a mouse tearing into cardboard boxes at midnight. She's very vivacious. She slaps his arm with a friendly tap, almost flirtatiously. My fury is strong. If she could see it, she'd be terrified. I know the power of my frown, which is not even a frown. From what I've been told, my gaze carries knives.

Even as I carry this look that might make a soul step aside, they don't look at me. Marcus is talking too candidly to her, smiling too much, answering her questions.

When I get there, I replace the brewing storm in my soul with a smile.

"Hey," I say, as if I just ran into him. I put my arm around his waist. "Hey baby." I kiss his cheek. "Sorry, we lost our seats. I needed to use the bathroom, too."

"Oh, I'm sorry," he says, blushing. I don't like that blush. It is almost as if I interrupted him. For once, I feel like dragging him out by the hair and ask for explanations. But I don't. As I hold him, I put my head on his chest, my hiding place. From there, I show the lass the storm in my eyes. She reacts to it.

"Oh, I'm sorry," she says to him, still smiling, but now nervously. "I guess I'll catch you later."

Catch you later?

I don't ask why she said that. I raise a smiling face at Marcus. "I'm sorry. I didn't mean to interrupt."

"Oh, you didn't interrupt anything. She works at the same office I work at," he says.

"Oh, now I understand the 'catch you later,'" I say.

"Yes, all to do with work."

"I see."

"You're going to use the bathroom?" he asks.

"Yes, very quickly. Will you wait for me?"

"Sure. I was thinking of seeing if we still have our spot, though."

"I doubt it," I say.

"Yeah, me too, but I might be able to snag another before someone else gets it."

I don't wish to argue. I don't want him to leave my side, but I also don't want him to think I'm chaining him.

"Sure, go for it," I say. "I'll be right back."

He leaves. I see him walk away before I get into the bathroom—which I don't need to use. I go in when he's out of sight, out of formality. I only wash my hands, then wait for a minute before making my way back.

When I leave the hallway, I look toward the bar. I spot him, quickly. He's talking to her again! I could fly to her and remove her life from her body in an instant, but that would dash everything I've worked for.

I could also walk to them, but decide to pause to listen. I drown out the music and the voices and focus on them. The music and the overall noise don't entirely disappear. They stretch and scatter till they get sparse and hollow, opening a path down which my auditory senses can travel.

"I loved the chocolates," she says, elbow on the bar, chin on her hand, overjoyed laughter in her mouth.

"I thought Joshua was jealous," Marcus laughs.

"Oh, who cares about Joshua!" She waves a dismissive hand. Her voice is almost sweet. "But did you mean it?" She looks keenly at him.

Marcus raises defensive hands. "Hey, let us not go there."

"Oh, come on! I wouldn't care. You know...I don't know if you'll get my drift...Sometimes we make mistakes."

Marcus points a finger at her. "Gotcha!"

"As to your other question. Maybe three?"

"Oh, that's a great number," Marcus replies. "I would love that."

This is all so confusing. Only *they* know what they're talking about, though there are some clues, and yet maybe they are not clues.

Music and noise come back to my ears.

She sees me approach and makes an excuse to leave. Marcus seems surprised, but turns as if he suspects something. He finally sees me and smiles.

Many thoughts come to me as we drive back. Many ideas. Maybe if we went together to another city, some place far away from the people we know. Yet we could still only be together at night, and living together is impossible unless he finds out about me and accepts the woman—the being— I've become. Only one thing could fix this, if he became like me. Even the ring of eternity, with its promise of immortality without death, does not promise eternity in happiness, nor does it does it guarantee faithfulness.

I think of all these things as he drives me back to my place—at least to my building, since he doesn't exactly know where I live. I wouldn't want him coming to my door to knock as I sleep.

Suddenly, red light. He looks at me. "Do you want children?"

The question is so abrupt it takes me by surprise.

"Children!" I exclaim.

"Yeah, children."

"Why do you ask?"

He shrugs, nonchalantly. "Just wondering. I would like children."

"You do?"

"Yes. Three."

"Three?"

"Too few? Okay, one million!"

I know he wants me to laugh, but I know it's a serious question. I feign humor. "One million! What about two billion?"

"A bit too many," he says with a laugh.

But I know he wants a true answer and that he expects me to reply. "I..." I pause. I don't know what to say. My womb is dead. *I* am dead. "I...I don't think it's the right time."

"Not the right time?" He seems surprised. His hand turns the steering wheel. We get on Sunset Blvd.

I don't answer. I look out the window with my hand on my chin. We pass by Kaiser Permanente.

"But do you want some?" he asks, suddenly.

I don't answer right away. "Yeah, sure," I say. "I hadn't thought of that."

"You hadn't?" He sounds shocked.

But it makes sense. To him thinking of children is the most natural thing in the world. He has said before he would like a large family, though he has never, till now, asked me a pointed question regarding that.

"Well, no," I say. "I wanted to live a long time without them. Just be with you. Until...Until things are better."

He nods, not toward me but at the road ahead.

He holds me before I go into my building. He leans back against his car and pulls me to him. Yet even as he does, even as he pecks my lips with sweet kisses and strokes my hair, I can sense something. My answer did not make him happy.

By the time he leaves, I'm in a dark place. I'm so angry I could shatter things. If I could resurrect Phillip, I'd kill him again. I'd show him my pain first, the pain of the beast—nay, the pain of the woman before he turned her into a beast and robbed her womb!

12

The pendulum

Instead of breaking things or killing someone—anyone who would annoy me at the moment, like my black neighbor—I walk like a normal human to Globe & Glass, my local liquor store. It's only two blocks away. One of the store's strengths is its selection of international drinks on its shelves. It's nearly ten minutes to two am when I get there and I rush for my spirits. First in line is a bottle of Jack Daniel's; next, a bottle of Morpheus brandy, then a Finnish vodka—the Leijona Viina—and a Jose Cuervo. If you've never mixed these together, I don't recommend it, unless you're a vampire.

"Drinking a lot tonight?" the young, friendly clerk—who looks like he just graduated from high school—asks me, arching an eyebrow as if with surprise.

It is almost two o'clock. If I don't want to kill him for canceling my order on account of the time—or just steal the bottles outright—I act a bit polite.

"Yes," I say. "Been a long night."

He smiles. "Yeah, I understand. When I get home I'll be poppin' in some of this poison myself. Helps you sleep."

I nod.

He concentrates on the cash register. "So, the grand total comes to a whopping one-hundred and five dollars and eighteen cents. Will that be cash or card?"

"Card."

"Came just in time," he says as he pushes some buttons so that I can scan my card. "But you're a regular, so I let it pass."

I know he wants me to thank him, but I just nod, feigning the speck of a smile.

"Receipt?"

I shake my head.

He puts my bottles in a bag and hands it to me. "Awesome. There you go, great lady of the night. Have a great day. Or a great night."

The 'great lady of the night' surprises me. But now that I have my things, I don't need to nod or say anything. I simply leave as if I didn't hear anything and I'm alone in the world.

As I sit and drink, waiting for the sun—my moon and my time to go to sleep—I think of ways to solve the issue of children—which comes right on top of solving the issue of darkness. I close my eyes a moment as if that will drown the pain—nay, my hate at my circumstances, my hate for Phillip, and my hate for me, for what I am.

Oh, turn the clock back, my soul cries.

"Oh, Phillip! You lied to me. You did not love me. You stole my soul. You hypnotized me into loving you. You drank my soul, not my blood. You drank my love, not my blood. You drank my mind, like you did my life. It was all for your selfish ends. Now I'm a monster!"

I try to erase the past. Even a vampire, with all his powers, cannot turn the dials to that moment when he could smile at the sun. I must think of ways to keep Marcus. How can I solve the child problem? If I turn him, turn him into the thing I hate about myself, what will that solve? Maybe I will stop hating myself if he becomes like me, but then...it will also be stealing his love. A thing stolen is not yours. My love is true because I loved him before I died. Would his be true if he stops loving me before he dies? There are so many things I need to save.

Finally, the dawn. I mournfully slip into my box. It's dark enough to stay awake a long time, and I do for an hour before I succumb to sleep.

Night arrives again. I call the gas station. I can't work today, not when so much is unsolved. Work doesn't give one enough time to think. If your life is crumbling, you need time to think. Work takes away the opportunity to do it in peace. I tell my boss I'm still not feeling well.

I go through the preparations to look good for Marcus again. I have a cold shower with scented soap. When finished, I go to the closet. I find a tight purple shirt and a black skirt. Then I look in the silver mirror, the only thing that will reflect my image. On goes the lipstick, the mascara, and the rouge. I'm still a form to which things can stick.

I throw on a long, dark-gray overcoat, spray perfume under and around it, and dab some behind my ears. I brush my wavy blond hair and recolor my nails.

We don't have plans to go out tonight, but I like to show up ready for anything, even if we only watch a movie on TV. My look might make him want to possess me again.

This time, I drive. I plan to look as normal as I can. I can make it home in time before dawn if I leave his place a little earlier. His small house is only twenty minutes away if you count traffic. It's quicker at three or four in the morning.

My drive is as uneventful as can be. Once, a driver hit me. We exchanged information and his insurance went up because of that.

To the world, I'm still alive, even to the government. When I get packages, they're left at my door, which I pick up at night. So far, no one has stolen them, which is a good thing. Even as a vampire, these little things of life—any deprivation of things you paid for with hard-earned money—can make your spirit get a human emotion.

My anger, of course, knowing of my powers, is deadlier than that of a human, and I have more resources to attain vengeance.

It takes me a moment to find parking. Once I get near Marcus's window, I vanish into thin air so I can observe him unseen. It is ten at night. He's not studying as usual, or sleeping. He's doing something I've never seen him do before: walk back and forth. He pauses from time to time to look pensively at the floor. What is he thinking about? He raises his eyes suddenly toward the corners of the ceiling. Then he closes his eyes and shakes his head.

I wish I had the power to break into his thoughts. He sighs as if a thought is torturing him. I cling to the idea—or clutch to it—that I'm *not* the reason for it, that our life is not the torture. If he feels tortured about something else, I'd like to know so I can help him, soothe him, comfort him.

Oh, my dear Marcus should not be suffering!

I'm wondering, should I make my presence known? I know we parted on good terms the night before, even if I sensed a mysterious vibration in his nervous system—one that, however, did not stop his arms from pulling me to him and making his body my home again, even while he drove away afterward.

I see him walk toward the bed. He picks up his phone from the bedside table and looks at it. He scrolls down some numbers and then pauses.

Suddenly, there is a buzzing vibration in my overcoat pockets—it is my phone, invisible though it is with me. Two seconds after the buzz, I hear: *When you call on me, when I hear you breathe, I get wings to fly, I feel that I'm alive!*

If not my body, my soul has a heart, and it shudders. I run away from the window. What reaction he has I don't know, but as I answer, he opens the door.

I am now visible and he sees me picking up the phone. He smiles and raises the phone to his mouth.

"Excuse me, where's my pizza?" he says."It's been over an hour. I don't think there'll be a tip for you *lass!*"

The heart in my soul laughs. My mouth is positively happy. My phone is already on my ear.

"Excuse me, sir," I reply into it. "But I think that mode of address is uncomely! I am a lady! I think we'll have to take the pepperoni off just for that."

"But it's a pepperoni pizza!" he says. "What are you going put on it—your undies? Your bra? Well, I might consider that then!"

"Ah! You obviously didn't hear me say I was a lady. Just for that, we'll be removing the cheese as well."

"No undies and no bra? And no cheese! Your ad says, 'for our customer's pleasure,' madam lass! I think you need to lose your job. This is ridiculous!"

His good mood immediately pulls me to his door. He immediately takes my hand and we go in.

"What's the occasion?" he asks as he closes the door.

"What do you mean?" I ask.

He looks me up and down. "You look like a CIA agent."

I laugh. "Oh, you mean the overcoat? I just thought I'd change into something more...elegant, I guess."

"Oh, I see. Well, it looks good on you."

He gets two beers out of the refrigerator.

I notice one thing: he didn't kiss me. He let me in as if I was just a friend. However, I don't make much of it, especially as there is naturalness in his demeanor. Maybe his deep thoughts, which he was walking around his bedroom, had nothing to do with me but something else. I feel a little more at ease.

Suddenly—just as I sit down with my beer—he hits me with it.

"Oh, I have great news. I'm going to Las Vegas. It's a school thing. I wanted you to come with me.

I shudder. "Come with you? To Las Vegas?"

"Yes, baby! What do you say?"

"What...What do I say?"

"Yes. Come on, what's there to think about? It will be great! A nice vacation for both of us."

"But...my work..."

"Yes, I know. I had thought of that. I have a solution. I've been thinking a lot about this, and this is the only way."

"What are you talking about? What...What solution?"

"The thing about your job. I don't like it. It's affecting us. I want you to quit."

"Quit! What do you mean?"

"That's it. I want you to quit. You don't need it. You have me."

"I have you?" I ask.

"Yes," he says.

"But...I like to be independent. At least a little."

"What do you mean 'independent?'" He raises his arms as if in disbelief. "People who love each other and are together are not 'independent' from each other."

I didn't think a man would have a problem with that word, but apparently Marcus does. I need to clarify.

"I mean...Not from you...I mean..."

"Look, darling, here's the thing: I'm tired of just seeing you at night. Not even at night—at two or three in the morning."

"I came earlier today," I say.

"Yes, but that's not always."

I feel I have to make my voice heard. "Marcus! I...I have bills!"

He only shrugs. "I'll take care of all that."

"But...You're not rich!"

"You mean you will only be with me if I am rich?"

Oh, he's really seeking to poke holes into the argument. That leaves me frustrated and almost without an answer. With all my powers, I still can't think straight.

"I...What? I am with you even though you're not rich!"

"That's not what I mean! Be with me *for real*, not just at three in the morning!"

"It is ten o'clock at night!" I literally raise my voice now.

"Why are you resisting?"

He almost yells this as he gets up and turns briefly before turning to me again. "I will pay for everything. It's about time! Do you love me?"

"More than you know."

"Then...let's do this! Hell, let us live together! I'm trying to find solutions here, for both of us. Fine, work if you want. I don't care. I just want us for once—*for once*—to wake up together! Look at the sun together."

All I can do is stare at him. He turns away from me again and leans on the refrigerator door. Then he turns back.

"Look, darling," he says. "I love you in your nice dresses, your nice make up, your nice hair, and everything else. You are so beautiful. I love all of that but...I can't remember the last time I saw you with a bad hair-day, with bags in your eyes, and just wearing pajamas. I miss that. I miss our morning coffees."

I'm sure he can see my face freeze.

"Is that really such a bad thing to ask?"

I shake my head. "No. Of course not." I understand but I still have to deflect from the topic. "But...Wait, you said Las Vegas?"

"Yes. Two weeks. We'll drive there. We'll leave early in the morning, after some breakfast, and be there by lunch. I think it'll be fun. You used to love roadtrips...not too long ago."

"What are you...We...Doing in Las Vegas?"

"My work is hosting a few events. I'm almost done with school. It will be a great opportunity to build connections. But that's not the only reason I want to go. We haven't done much together. Not like we used to." He sits on his heels and holds my cold hands warmly. "I miss my old Adelia." He kisses my cold fingers.

The pendulum seems to go to the other side and I can't stop it.

This thirst in me to keep him alive is also for me to feel alive. If he only wore the ring of eternity, which he is *still* not wearing, we could... No, we couldn't. Trevor was right. The ring requires knowledge of us, the only way for it to be effective.

Though the ring would keep Marcus alive forever—keep him from aging—it doesn't secure his eternal love for me unless he *knows* of me, which is what the vow intended to do. But I also wanted to protect Marcus, just in case he didn't accept who we are. Especially who *I* am. This is why Trevor asked him the questions he did.

Marcus's ignorance of who I am is just as bad as he finding out *who* I am. Both things threaten my happiness. My inability to spend the daytimes with him is as likely to drive him away as his knowledge that I need to kill to live.

I have to do something. The thought of striking his neck with my fangs is often strong. It would be the only time I did this without anger or hunger, only with love. But then— what would he be, who would he be? He might not be the same Marcus.

I tell him that I will think about this—I tell him, even, that there is a *ninety-nine point-nine, point-nine, point-nine percent* chance I'll go with him.

I have much to think about as I drive back home.

13

Henry Tubald

I come to Trevor with questions. He greets me as he always does.

"Lovely Adelia, the moon in your eyes is dark. What ails you?"

As always, he is sitting by the fire, a bottle of wine on the tea table. I came in as I always do, through the walls. I did not have to knock. I have eternal invitation into his abode.

"You can always see trouble in my face," I say.

"Darkness is hard to hide. It's only what is inside it that must be revealed."

"I'm afraid to say you were right. He...He is wearing the ring... And..." No he is not, but I have to lie. I don't want to reveal all my failures.

"There is a *but* and not an *and* there," he says.

"You are right." There is a chair near his, and I sit down.

"It's why the vow was important, though I understand your fears. He probably puts on the ring, takes it off, puts it in a drawer, without thinking much about it."

"I'm sorry to have offended the honor of Mantheluse."

"Mantheluse will deal with itself. Be comforted that the spirits cannot touch the living, especially as there were no secrets revealed. He is safe from us, but you are not safe from him."

Trevor is an intriguing figure. I feel that he's caught my lie and is willing to let it slide. Or maybe he doesn't believe it is completely a lie. All the same, he's caught the scent of half of it.

"You wanted to protect him because you love him," he continues. "If only he knew the depths of your love."

"He wants me to...to quit my job. To live with him in the daytime."

Trevor looks at me—not sweetly, but contemplatively.

"Yes, he is human," he says at length. "Sweet Adelia, this is a hopeless love."

I get up and cover my face with my hands. "I can't believe it!"

"Your pain shakes every tomb—it makes all the dead tremble."

"Why do I feel like this? Why am I not *with* him as I am with others? I am dead, am I not? I am a monster, am I not? How—why am I cursed with love? Why can I not love the tomb of my coldness?"

"Because you were deprived of that love when alive. Your life never died, only your body. Love is a life, and memory is its blood. Memory is not just a thought. It is a sensation. A feeling. Remember grandpa the ghost? He is as dead as a coffin six-feet under. Yet he still carries his love around his old house for those he cherished in life. All vampires are unique. Your commonality with others is your uniqueness. Don't think your story is new. Yours is just one of the most powerful. Yours does not give up. You still want to ride that horse you used to ride as a child. A dead rider, who comes back to life, wants to love every horse he sees."

I can see the metaphor. I am like that rider that died. My horse is called Love. Love is what I loved, and Marcus is the representation of that love I lost. I am simply trying to get it back, because I can't believe that I lost him when I died.

"It's best to let the living die," I hear from somewhere. There suddenly appears Henry Tubald in his ascot and high collared shirt, waistcoat, and black polished shoes, holding a flower to his nose like a dark debonair. "But now I understand, and I am sorry I was not more ingratiating with him." He smiles a sweet smile at me. "Lovely Adelia, what can I say? Sometimes the best thing—the most noble thing to do—is to leave alone the blooming rose. Let it rise and die. Smell it once and don't take it home. Let it live, thrive, and wilt on its own. That is how beautiful things die. They carry their scent with them, but we remember it as a beautiful dream. Let life die, I say. We can still be happy in darkness with our own kind. There is *not* too much darkness in us even if we live in a dark world. We are monsters and lovers, as you yourself show, but we can be lovers to ourselves and to the things that make more sense. Your hands are cold but vibrant." He takes my hands. "They're warm in our world. Why don't you give the immortal heart a chance, a heart that cherishes what you represent, without secrets? We can also love, and our love is less dying." He lets go of my hands now but keeps his eyes on me. "It lasts a little longer. Life, on the other hand, does not last. It must die. It does not become us except through terror and pain. What do you say, why don't you give darkness a chance? There is a home in it." He takes my fingers now. "Why don't you come with me? Let us take a flight into the night. Let us go to the moon. Why, laughter is not dead if the soul has breath, even if the body is cold with death."

"Gentle Henry Tubald—or should I call you Gentle Romeo?—you give poetry to our plight. I appreciate the offer, but I'm willing to dig this tomb till my body sinks in it." I take my fingers back and curtsy.

Henry laughs. "You do yourself great harm. As I said, the nobility of the heart is in letting go. Of course, I don't imply letting go of everything. Just the things that hurt us and that we will hurt in the end. By saving them from ourselves, we save ourselves from them. I can see us, you and I, two winter embers who only need a little oxygen to reveal their fire. That oxygen is chance—the giving of the opportunity. You and I can be those embers that opportunity blows into existence."

"Oh, Henry," I reply. "How could you love one like me?"

"To say that I love you, sweet Adelia, would be a truth and a lie. Love is a progression. One must love the thought of someone before one can love his or her company. Now, you can make of it what your heart tells you. The point is, I am offering an alternative where you can be happy and not in torture."

Henry is handsome and an important member of this court of vampires. I myself am only an invitee to the circle, a honored title, and so my presence is never questioned, especially because of my friendly relations with its greatest member, Trevor Luccan.

"Lord Henry," I say, curtsying again, even bowing—my address is somewhat a mockery, since he and I are on friendly terms, but also a sign of my respect for his good intentions. "I thank you for your good counsel—and for your offer—but there may be other cures to my pain, such as will give me all I want, preserve my passion, and immure me from too much pain."

Henry soundlessly laughed at my address, and yet seemed to like it.

"Only doing what your passion prohibits you from doing will immure you from greater pain. And yet you will steal a life the same way yours was stolen."

Oh, this man knows how to launch a spear. It splinters the very heart of my resolve to find a solution to my pain. For it is true I am viscerally against gaining my Marcus through such an act as turning him. Indeed, if Marcus only knew the depths of my love!

Henry suddenly throws himself on his knees, presents his hand to me.

"Sweet Adelia, accept this love, this invitation, to learn further of what your heart is capable of."

He looks quite adorable as he says this, for I am still a woman who can blush at words of desire. Respecting of his status in our court, I also kneel. I take his hand.

"Dear Henry, I accept your love as an idealization of what might be—as the spirit of the stranger you envision before she accepts your graces and tenderness in a different manner. Then she might fly to the moon with you. Today, she flies to the earth."

Henry says, "You've made up your mind, then, to keep digging this grave where your own body might fall."

I try to speak, candidly. "This shovel that digs this grave might in the end find a jewel. But we will see. I don't know how far I will go. I only need a chance to see. For now, my windows are shuttered, and my door held closed, though with a stone. I will kick the stone if my need for a different future arises." I get up. He grasps my hand again, still on his knees.

"All my chambers are open, a permission eternally granted to cross their threshold anytime you wish, whenever you need companionship, whether for a night or for eternity."

"Thank you, Henry. I will always prize you as a noble lord and an honest lover. Now leave me to my pain. Goodbye now."

While Henry and I have never been together, it's obvious he is a little jealous of others' attentions toward me. Yet, he has always been respectful, even sometimes teasing, and always elegant.

14

Mother

Power is lost when you love. I, who can fly six hundred miles in an hour, a deadly predator, with greater strength in my arms than a harpy eagle, who can carry a thousand-pound object to the highest mountain, am powerless against Marcus.

Trevor has demystified some of this conundrum. He compared Marcus once to a parent figure—one who, though old, still exerts the power of authority over his children, to whose demands they still acquiesce, though they're stronger.

I see clearly what he means. It is the human in me—the remnant of it—that weakens me. What I do outside it is simply a method of survival, not part of the nature of the monster, even while others might see it that way.

And so I am caught between these two spirits. Yet my human spirit does not make me human, and that is what causes the pain. It's like being in a room where my eyes look out the window. Marcus brings the sun, even while, wrapped in his arms—his dear arms—I cannot fully partake of it. I am *with* it, but separated from it.

Unwilling to face Marcus and his insistence that we move in together, I decide to keep away for a while. After a few days of absence from work, I am lucky I still have a job. It becomes my escape—what it was not before. Till now, it had only been my excuse. Now it's a place where I can put my thoughts together. I only call Marcus to remind him of my existence, though even that is risky. He brings up the subject again, though he is not as insistent as he would be if we were in the same room. He only says, "Have you thought of what we talked about?" I answer, "Yes, I have."

On day two of my absence from his house, I bring up my mother, whom I've not seen in over a year. I instinctively use her as an anchor, saying that she wants me to visit her. I can tell his disappointment through his silence.

After our goodbyes, I quickly call my mother—not to reconnect, since I find nothing in common with her—but to get her into the game of my lie.

She is happy to hear from me.

"Oh, my darling! My sweetheart! Oh, my good heart! You're calling me! Did you change your number? I haven't been able to reach you."

My voice is a bit cold. "Yes, Mother. I'm sorry about that."

"Oh, but why?"

"Oh, you know. Things happen."

"It's okay. At least you called. Finally. How are you, Sweetheart?"

"I am okay. Listen, I haven't seen you in a while," I say.

"Oh, I know darling! But...you sound troubled."

I can tell that my voice has given her pause. I reshape my tone, since I need her.

"Oh, no, Mother. I'm still at work and...and it's chilly. Maybe that's why."

"Oh, I see. I understand. I miss you so much! When are you going to come? I'll throw a party! So many people want to see you."

"Oh, no," I say. "I just...want to spend time with you. Nobody else."

"I see, why is that?"

"Oh, Mom, I have to work. Listen, if Marcus calls you, tell him we set up to meet on the fifteenth. Please."

"On the fifteenth. Eh...Okay? Sure. I guess. Why not. Is everything okay between you and Marcus?"

"Yes, it's all dandy. I just...Listen...I can't go on his trip with him. Personal reasons. He's disappointed about that."

"A trip?"

"Yes, he's going on a trip. I can't talk too much. Everything is okay between us. Please tell him that."

She seems to catch the fact that I'm using her as a subterfuge. I reassure her that I was planning to see her, and that our priorities—Marcus's and mine—are at odds. She seems to believe me.

We chat a bit longer than I plan, but it makes her feel good. In a way, it makes *me* feel good, too. Trevor is right. There are people that we honor, instinctively, dead or alive. Mother is someone I'd never hurt, since she was always kind to me, even if I have changed. Even in my undeath, I find ways to talk to people as if I were alive—though perhaps it all has to do with Marcus.

The morning of the fifteenth, I sit at my lonely table, waiting for dawn. I begin to see the clear of the approaching daylight through the sides of my black curtains. I so long to peek outside before the sun is fully up, but I fear that even *that* would be dangerous. I want to touch the light, even if it fills me with blisters and reminds me of who I am. I gaze at the silvering from a distance, without approaching the window, even as my curiosity is deep.

My heart has been crying, and it overflows with the silvering light. By now Marcus is likely up, putting his luggage in the trunk of his car, or having breakfast and the coffee he wishes to have with me.

As I wait for the ray that will force me into my closet, into my box-bed, where I will sleep till the sun is down, I take the last swill of my Morpheus brandy. When night falls again, I am lonelier than ever. My curiosity to see the early morning, however, has provoked a mysterious itch in me: to reach a part of a life I've been absent from—my old home. It is an extension of the part of day I'm now foreign to, even if my visit occurs during moonlit hours.

I don't get ready the same way I would for Marcus, but I do my best to look like the figure of the past my mother is acquainted with.

Mother's house is 150 miles away. I get there in fifteen minutes, quite a long flight. After materializing and inspecting through the windows to make sure there is no one in the house other than my mother—my father, an old attorney, died a few years ago, before my own death—I ring the old bell. It is nine o'clock.

Mother does something I don't expect when she opens the door: she hugs me. There are tears in her eyes. I have a strong urge to separate from the warm embrace, but allow it, not wanting to push her away, feeling that I have to honor her and not hurt her—which a sudden forward motion of my arms could do by sending her flying to the other side of the room.

Indeed, she looks so foreign to me. She takes me into the house by holding my hand, saying that I shouldn't be out in the cold too long because it is bad for my health.

I'm thoroughly unacquainted with the proper way to act with a human who shows such emotion for me. Only with Marcus do I feel confident in this regard. I feel his chest is my home.

Maybe it's not my death that causes the impulse to retreat and reject the warmth she offers, but the distance we have accumulated—not only physical but emotional—through a long separation. Then again, maybe it has to do with the fact that I'm a vampire, deprived of the motor that creates human connection. Oh, the curse of death!

It is confusing in a way why I am different with Marcus. He is also part of my past, and yet the one thing I refuse to relinquish, to let go. Why this discrepancy, I don't know.

Mother offers me coffee. I decline with a simple no, without even a *thank-you* at the end of the decline. I almost feel like I made a mistake in coming. So detached I am from this sphere and the warmth she offers. I treat her like one of my customers at the gas station who tries to engage me.

All the same, I feel I need to take something from here. Some picture of lost experiences—the way one would take a memory through an object representative of where you've been.

Just as I did over the phone, I shift my tone and rework my gaze to look warmer. The success of this effort is not plain till her own eyes replace their wonder at my coldness with a smile. We are sitting in the living room.

"Your old friend Rosalind was here a few days ago. Asked me about you."

"Oh?" I say.

"I told her you were fine but that you had moved far away. By the way, where did you park?"

"Me? Oh...I...I took the bus."

"The bus! Child, it is a hundred and fifty miles from L.A! How on earth did you find a bus to bring you here?"

Terrible error. For some reason, this has made me human. A human needs to defend himself, unlike a vampire who owes no explanations to anyone.

I look up as if I'm trying to recall my bus trip. "Well, I went to the station, asked some questions, and I'm suddenly here."

Mother seems to want to laugh but stops trying to probe. She gives reasons why.

"Well, I don't care how you got here. I'm so happy you're here. Too bad you don't want anything."

"No. I'm not hungry. I just wanted to see you."

"I've been dying to see you. You see how emotional I got? After your disappearance—I don't mean to bring back those days, just to say that my world almost ended. I don't know how you could do that. I don't know what I would have done if...But I'm glad you just moved, though I don't know why you wouldn't tell me. Was someone keeping you, telling you not to call us?"

"I don't want to talk about it," I say.

Mother nods, though she seems uncomfortable. It seems like all she wants is my presence and would not threaten it for the world with unnecessary, uncomfortable questions.

"Oh, you like the drapes? I changed them to your favorite color, yellow, like the sun."

She points at the curtains, inviting me to look.

I liked yellow?

I look at them. "They're nice."

"Come on, have some coffee, at least. Or would you prefer wine?" She laughs somewhat at the end of this. "I know you're old enough now. I won't be put in jail for that."

"Who would put you in jail?" It looks like I've lost a link even to old jokes as well, though I don't realize this right away.

Mom waves her hand. "Oh, I'm joking, silly! I wouldn't be put in jail. And we knew you were drinking at eighteen, so it's not like I don't know you drink. But as long as you stayed safe and responsible, we didn't care. We just wanted you safe."

She still speaks as if my father was around, though this I can understand. It's hard to close the door on your memories, even the dear ones whose absence hurts you. Hearing her talk like that, I look at her, and even feel a bit closer. She *would* return to Dad too if she died and resurrected. Why wouldn't she? I find her a kindred spirit, suddenly.

My mind goes far away, thinking of Dad. When I return, it is as if the whole conversation has been about him and I reach my hand to her. "Everything will be alright."

She's surprised at this. She doesn't understand it, and I don't push her to understand because I think she soon will.

Suddenly, I look around.

"You know this is your home, right? It has never stopped being your home, whenever you want to come back, if you ever do."

I look at her again. Her words surprise me. She's welcoming me into her home. For some reason, it makes me a little warmer. It was also my home at one point. It's the home where I grew up.

I don't say *thank-you* here, either, but look around again. I take in the sight of the place. I take in the memory that once was. My eyes fall on an image. It's a picture in a small table. I get up without saying anything and approach it.

There is man in the picture. There is a girl. And next a woman. It is my mother. I pick up the picture. I don't even notice Mom standing by me.

"That is such a lovely picture," Mom says. "You were thirteen. Oh, your father. He loved you so much."

As she talks I stare at the picture. I stroke it with my hand.

"My father," I say, almost with a whisper.

Mother can hear me. "Yes," she says.

"He never came back."

"No, darling. But his spirit is always here. And he is in your heart and mine."

I look at her. "He's with me."

"Always, sweetheart."

I look at the picture again. "This is me," I say, almost with surprise.

"Yes," Mom says again. "And that is me. We took that in San Diego."

Oh, the sun is coming. I begin to feel it. It is warm. I close my eyes. Try to remember the pictures. The images of my life.

"Oh, Dad," I say, suddenly, opening my eyes, caressing the face in the picture.

"Mom, this is you!" I exclaim, as if I just discovered it.

"Yes, darling. That's me."

I turn to her.

"Oh, you don't need to cry," she says.

"Cry!" I exclaim.

"Yes," Mother says. "They are little tears. Welcome back home, sweetheart."

This is a weight on me. It oppresses my soul as if it had a chest. I realize now—though my eyes don't shed normal tears—how I can show the trace of the thing that once formed them.

I put the picture down. I look around again.

"What is it, darling?" Mom asks.

"Where is my bedroom?"

"Oh, you forgot? Right over here, sweetheart."

She leads me to my bedroom. There is my bed. It is made. Around are teddy bears. There's a dollhouse on the dresser. There is my closet. Then...there is the window!

Oh, no! The memories. Terrible. I get angry as I look at it. All my life, all my dreams, were dashed because of it. Right there—right outside of it—is where stood the thief—the thief of my blood, of my soul, of my life. It is *he* who gave me my pain—Phillip! My fangs almost come out at this moment. I am happy Mom is behind me, or she'd be terrified. I feel such hate, I could shatter the window. I see Phillip again. Memory comes back to me of what he did!

I fall to my knees, close my eyes and hold my head to stop the memory.

Mother becomes worried. "Darling, what is it?" she asks, coming down to hold me.

"I have to go!" I say. I get up. I don't even give her time to follow me as I'm out the door in an instant. When I'm out of view, I disappear and fly back into the night, never wanting to set foot in my old home again!

15

A Heart in Twilight

Is there a ring that will allow you to walk in sunlight? I conclude there isn't, or Trevor would be wearing it.

I fear I will turn into a monster. There are some positive thoughts regarding it. While Marcus and I would be restricted to moonlight romances, it would be eternal, and it could still be sweet—sweet to sit by the waves on a large ocean rock. Yet the price of this is his own blood. His own sun. Why would I do what Phillip did to me?

So I loved my captor, the thief that stole my sun. Then I woke up and realized what he had done. Had I woken up before the other vampire killed him, I might have killed him myself. Oh, how easy love can turn to hate when you see the whole picture!

Yet I am also guilty of the sin that transformed me. I also steal suns on my midnight hunts. How am I different? Perhaps because I kill my prey. There is no suffering once you're truly departed. The few I've turned into vampires pleaded through their suffering to be vampires. I, on the other hand, was not suffering when I was turned. I was happy.

I wouldn't have to be a thief if I was a full member of the vampire court—or I accepted Henry Tubald and became his consort. The court members still kill now and then, to be sure, but they don't need to. Blood is offered to them in golden goblets to quench their blood hunger.

In the vampire world, we don't quench thirst, but hunger.

The next few nights are almost peaceful. I don't understand. My comfort comes, I guess, from the fact that I still have Marcus, even if he is far away. I laugh with him over the phone. He tells me he wishes I was there with him. Tells me of the parties he's been to. He suddenly also stops asking me whether I've thought about moving in with him.

I don't think much of it. He's likely given up. At least for now. I'm certain it will come up again. Right now, he's giving it time.

Next two nights, 11 pm. He doesn't call me and he doesn't answer the phone. I panic the first time, but he calls me at 3 am to say good-night. The second night, I call him, and leave a message. He doesn't return the call.

I don't give it much thought. Considering his 3 am call the first time, I conclude he's fallen asleep.

Next few days. No calls. No return to my messages. On the last day of his trip, he calls me at three in the morning.

"Hey, baby. I got a job offer," he says.

"Oh, darling, that is fantastic!" I say.

"Yes, but...good news and bad news," he says.

"What are the good and bad news?"

"Well, the good news is that it is with an important law firm. They're very confident I'll pass the bar, and have offered me a job. That's gonna be good for me. They'll start me off with a hundred-fif-ty-K a year."

"Oh, wow, that is so excellent! We can buy a lot more wine with that!"

He doesn't laugh. Instead, he says, "Oh, yes, the bad news, though, the job is in Tennessee."

Here I almost drop the phone.

"What the *fuck* are you talking about!" I exclaim.

"Oh, come on baby, you know how these things are. That's life. Sometimes...you want someone to share it with you. Your ups and downs. Your successes and your failures. I don't want to stay fixed in one place. But listen. I *know* you want to talk more, but I can't right now. I...I'll maybe call you later."

He hangs up. My spirit has a nose because it is breathless.

The bars are closed, and the liquor store doesn't sell alcohol past two am. The only things I have are my drinks, which are running low.

Since Marcus went on this trip I've had no clue what to do with myself. At least I've had Trevor to dissipate my sense of loneliness. I don't even dare show my face to him now with my new troubles.

I feel like taking someone's life in my anger. A terrible urge in my nature—the urge to steal suns. Let not my neighbor knock on my door tonight! I'd swiftly take him to a mountain! I close my eyes—put more darkness in my world to dissipate my violent thoughts.

The drinks douse my spirit as I once again await the peeking of the silvering dawn.

Many nights arrive again, this time without Marcus's phone calls. Every night, I fly by his place. He's not home yet. I fly dizzily around my world—limited though the space be for a vampire who must make sure not to travel too far lest the sun suddenly wakes up and looks at you—and you, in your despair, didn't see it coming.

For almost four—nay, five—weeks, I've foregone nurture of my body just to behave as Marcus would want a future bride to behave. That's the human in me still palpitating in my carcass. My love has been my destruction in so many ways. I'm hungrier than ever now. The shred of the human nature I've tried to hold on to is disappearing. I feel terror of who I'm becoming. I'm melting with tearless despair.

To stop me from becoming a monster—despite my troubles and the inner nature that prod me to be one—I fly to Trevor's place. He's there as usual. His damsels of the night are with him, sitting on the couch, not talking, simply looking at him. Next to them, however, are the goblets filled with the nourishment I seek. Today, however, I seek more than just blood.

"Lovely Adelia," he says as I appear. "Oh, those clouds. They're increasing."

I don't reply this time. Rather, I kneel before him and look down. I hear him close his book, which shows he is surprised.

"Please allow me to be a part of your court," I say. I close my eyes and lay my hand on my chest.

He doesn't speak for a moment. I don't interrupt his silence. He's likely trying to put his thoughts together.

Suddenly, he says, "There are only two ways to become a part of our court. One of those ways you have rejected."

"What is the other way?" I ask. "I'll do anything."

He is silent again. I wait.

At last he speaks. "The other way is layered. One of those layers requires moral integrity. That you have. You honor the people who once were close to you. In our court, we kill only out of necessity, with only a few liberties now and then. The less you kill, the safer we are as immortals. Like the living world, we also seek peace. I do think you pass those tests. The other is elegance. You like to dress well. Your rectitude, even in your suffering, is the mark of a great spirit. Next is the recommendation of at least seven members. That is the most difficult part. You could say we engage in immortal politics. The last one is monetary. Not because we need the money, but because money allows us to maintain our blood supply, in a legal way, without the need to hunt."

Here I look at him. This surprises me.

"It's not as much as you think," he says, as if trying to reassure me. "How you get that money, we don't care, as long as you don't get caught. You have a way to do it the legal way, the world thinks you're alive. You can get into investments, get a profitable nighttime job. Things like that."

"How much?" I ask.

"Twenty thousand a month."

Make it a million! I think.

"It's not as difficult as you think," Trevor continues. "If it was all up to me, I'd make you a member now. However, if I did, there would be a revolt. The court would lose its prestige, since everyone has had to do what I just said to become a member."

"All the members began that way?" I ask.

"No, not the first members, of course." He sighs, suddenly. "Believe it or not, most vampires don't qualify for the honor of belonging to our noble coven—our vampire court. "You, on the other hand, ever since I first set eyes on you, lovely Adelia, are different. There was a different soul in you, which is why, with my power, made you into an honorary member. For the full membership, however, to have all you like, all that I say is required. You have already fulfilled some of that. The other would be to become a soul maiden to a member. That is indeed the easiest way."

I know he can see my face of frustration and disappointment, even as I hide it in a mask of composure—or try, at least.

He suddenly says, looking at me, "You are paler than usual. You've been starving yourself." He reaches for a goblet near him. "Here, have this," he says. He's offering me his own drink.

I take the goblet with both my hands and drink. Though I try decorum, I'm sure I appear ravenous as I imbibe.

"There," he says. "That should keep you. It is not good to starve yourself, lovely Adelia."

When I get back to my apartment, nourished by Trevor's generosity with his own blood—at least the one in the goblet, not *his* exactly—I can face my black neighbor who appears again on his way to his own apartment. He gives me a cold look as he passes by and shakes his head. Once he is out of sight, I get into my door. My chair at my table waits for me, and I sit to wait for the dawn again.

Yet I can't sit in peace. *Twenty-thousand dollars!* I reflect. *A month!* I only make twenty-three-hundred after taxes. How to acquire such a sum? I feel so divided from both the human and spirit world, all of a sudden.

I am in pain. My dear Marcus is angry. Is he rethinking us? Oh, no—I can't think of it! It would tear me if he were to tell me goodbye. What spiral would I fall into? What vortex of pain?

Twenty-thousand-dollars a month, I reflect again. The sum is my oasis from thoughts of Marcus—from the fears that my position brings with him. Yet it is still debilitating on my spirit. How can I come up with that? The cost to live a civilized death is high.

As I think of this, I go back to my phone. Marcus is absent. He hasn't called me. I am in so much pain. But at least I'm fed, so all I have are the thoughts of my suffering in love, and in hatred for Phillip!

The next night, I finally get what I've been thirsting for. Marcus calls me. He tells me he is on his way back, that he will be home by three in the afternoon. He tells me he wants to have lunch with me, to talk. He diverts the topic as I ask for explanations about his not calling me.

"Oh, it's a long, convoluted story. Can you make it for lunch?"

"I...I can meet you after work," I say.

"Yeah, I figured."

He sounds disappointed again.

"I told you it's all I can do," I say. I touch my cheek. I'm crying.

"I understand. What time? At three?"

"I...You know, I need to save money. I have...Yes, I need to work. I would like to leave early but..."

"No, I understand." I can hear him sigh through the phone. "I'll see you at three then. I have to go now. Bye."

"Wait, that's it?"

"I got things to do. Just...Come at three."

"Ok," I say.

"Ok, ciao," he says and hangs up.

Keep your honor, I say—because I want to hit someone. You can have both Marcus and the court, if you concentrate.

16

Revelations

Marcus has a lover! Henry Tubald has just told me all about it at Trevor's place, where I went once again to seek Trevor's counsel. Henry spotted him at the mall at seven in the evening, when the sun was already down. Henry was out shopping for a new tie and an expensive cologne that he had seen advertised—which apparently drives mortal dames crazy—when he happened to come across Marcus—who was wearing the ring of eternity—and some brunette piece of trash!

A brunette! A brunette! Oh, no! The girl from the bar! His co-worker. His trip of two weeks! His unanswered calls. That can *only* be her. She's living blood! How could I not think she would be at those work-hosted events?

Oh, no! My dear, loving Marcus would not do this to me! It's impossible! No, this is a lie! This is a lie! Marcus would not do this to me! No, no! He's a dear soul! He loves me! He's shown me he loves me! Dearly loves me! Just like I love him! But then, the phone calls, his silence, his talk of children and us moving in together!

"Are we over, dear Marcus?" I say. "If so, why not tell me to my face! Tell it to my face, you coward!" I scream the last words.

I'm spiraling out of control.

What do I do now? What do I do? These are my questions. First, I feel betrayed. Second, heartbroken. Even understanding, yes! How could I think that Marcus would be faithful to me when we see each other less than half the time that even bad lovers spend together?

But I've had to make sacrifices so that he could love me. It has required keeping a job and a roof over my head. To look alive! He has been wanting to keep me, telling me to move in together, enjoy morning coffees with him! How could I show him *me* in the daytime?

She can give him that!

Of course, I do not go to work. My spirit is too depressed, my mind too angry, my heart too broken. I do not even want to see him, for fear of making a mistake, becoming a monster, becoming violent. I would lose all hope of having Marcus as *Marcus*! I have to think of a way to fix this. I call upon myself, upon whatever strength I have left, to be understanding, conciliatory. But I cannot let him have his girlfriend. She must be out of the way. I concoct plans. Terrible plans.

But the betrayal! Not one second after I've chosen understanding, I become violent again—not against this new girl, but against him. I cry my plasmatic tears again.

I need a drink. It needs to be strong. I go to my cupboard, which I'm not sharing with Marcus because that would require mornings with him. I realize this as I bring down the brandy, the whiskey and the tequila. I will mix them all in a large cup. It will be pungent, burning. I will feel it. The blood in me gives me sensations and feelings. The blood I drank nearly twenty weeks before is still in me, I'm sure of it. It came from a wise man, but a depressed man. It would make sense. Depressed people think a lot. They're poets. They unravel the mysteries of life in their pain, can see what others can't. Some of it is wisdom, the rest a fog of confusion, of weakness, of lack of determination. It is that, perhaps, which has drawn me to the drinks and to my holding myself back for the moment, and to reflect on what the right path is.

The wise man's blood mixes with the blood from the girl from eight weeks ago. She was a girl in distress, broken-hearted because a man cut short his promise of eternal love. I had such pity for her. I was inclined to make her immortal. But I didn't want a companion. I wanted what I had, and nothing else. She will be found in the river when her body finally surfaces.

Oh, demons clutch me! I can't think straight. My spirit needs a triage. With my violent thoughts and my confusions holding me back, I wager I'd be first in line.

Yes, definitely first in line.

Bottoms up. Potent alcohol. My tongue has life. It can taste. The drink burns its coldness. Is that a tingling I feel on my tongue?

Her blood reacts, and her emotions come to me the way she might have felt when she had a bit too much. So, it's not a walk in the park, or an easy flight among the clouds under a clear and peaceful moon, to have such a many-formed hooch in a twenty-four ounce cup. Except for the even gait, my still good sight, hearing, smelling, etc. I am drunk. Vampires feel the drink in their emotions, not in their walk.

I'll sit down and watch TV. There is a vampire series I've been meaning to watch for a while. The directors know absolutely shit about the immortal world! They paint us vampires as if we have feelings similar to those of the mortals. What a crock!

All I can feel is being filled up by the alcohol. I'm as healthy dead as the best hope. After poisoning the blood I received from Trevor's goblet in such a way, the only blood I'll have for two or three weeks perhaps—at least the liquor's spirit evaporates even in a vampire—I am such a mess of feelings. But I refuse to go see Marcus.

I stay away. I can't think clearly with these heart-rending feelings, with this drunkenness of my spirit and my emotions, of my self-control! I do not want to regret it. I hold myself back. I hold myself back. I am chained. Incapacitated. I go far away. Far away. I fly. I fly. Go over the clouds. Away from the direction that leads me to Marcus. I cannot do it. I must relax. I will be home before the sun comes up. I am indeed back. Barely made it to my oasis, but I'm so stressed I can barely close my eyes, even when I know that my morning death is gripping my bones, my senses. Finally, I rest. Finally, I sleep.

17

Broken Vows

I did not go to Marcus yesterday because I was afraid to regret what I would do if his infidelity was true. So, I suffered alone and got my spirit drunk. But today, I must know. I can't live forever wondering, pretending I'm not wounded or jealous while the worm eats me from within. But many things stop when I rise in the evening. The darkness is painful. Palpitating. It has a heart, and it beats oppressively against my chest, against my temples. It's an earthquake. Strange feeling for someone dead like me.

I can't go to work. Surely this is the feeling of my broken-hearted victim, who told me that life without the man she loved was death, and that she feared to be dead. Such is what I fear. I fear to be dead. I've never wanted to be part of the dark world. A part of death. But Henry Tubald was ready to remind me that I was different.

My death feels more succinct, now, like the curtain is closing at last, sending me from night's sunlight into night's dark. The only reason besides love that I have lived the way I have lived has been to taste the life Phillip deprived me of. It's like I was never meant to be dead, and my spirit rebels, wants to insist on being alive.

It's a tantrum, like that of a baby refusing to have his toy taken away. I rather he had sent me into eternal unconsciousness, for the living dead feel a pain unlike any pain. Hopelessness descends quickly like the lid of the coffin, closing on everything. It drops the universe's darkness onto us, erases roads, loves, things to touch, mouths to kiss.

I don't know what cries in me. I feel it in my stomach, and I bend over as if someone kicked out my oxygen. I'm a mess. For a dead woman, I'm a mess! I dare not look in the mirror. I'd see an ugly face. Yet what I fear most is what I would not see: human tears, but tears that remind me of who I am. I want no reminders that I'm not alive—that my flight in the air is my bicycle, my sun the moon.

Anger and curiosity push away some of the terror of my darkness. Now I'm jealous and curious. It is nine p.m. I'm supposed to be working, but I sacrifice this pretense of life for the chance to be a witness of my own death. I fly—I would drive or take the bus to feel alive, because I still feel the need to—but I need to get to Marcus' place, quickly.

I land on the roof like a proper bird of prey on a neighbor's roof that gives me view of his porch. He is sitting on a chair. Oh, yes, he's with her! The brunette—the same girl from the bar. His co-worker.

She plays with his hands. She looks at the ring on his right hand, the ring that binds him to me, eternally; meshes her fingers with his, smiles. She approaches his body between his legs and throws her arms around his neck. Sickening sweetness! Betraying sweetness!

I gave him all my love. I can't help that the night was not enough, that my kisses were not enough. Why wear the ring if he didn't mean to be faithful—eternally faithful? I was a fool. And yet he loved me. He loves me. But...I am not enough. The night is not enough. The moon is not enough. Despite the clubs and bars, the late dinners, we did not live as a pair. We had no relationship, only a rendezvous. I'm already speaking in past tense. Maybe I can save it.

They kiss.

I can't take this anymore! Oh, anger! Oh, fangs! Violence is a storm in me. And yet...

I wait. I want to strike the roof but stay still. I vanish again and appear from the darkness into the light. Up he stands when I appear. She moves away. Just as Marcus begins to open his mouth to explain himself, I vanish. She jumps to his arms, terrified, clings to him like a child to a parent's leg and closes her eyes like she's in a wild ride.

Marcus is not terrified. He is stunned and mystified. He leaves her standing alone on the porch, and comes down the steps.

"Adelia, I saw you," he says.

I say nothing. I begin to walk away. My fury is in my heart. I pick up rock I see on the ground and throw it with violence at the window of his house. I shatter the pane. Now the poor girl is in a panic. She calls Marcus back. Even Marcus doesn't know where the hell the rock came from. But she is losing it.

"Marcus, come back!" she cries.

Marcus the knight in shining armor protects her. He takes her at the waist and disappears with her into the door. I cannot go in now. The door is closed. Why is this so in the vampire world? Humans need to release us from it. It's the morality of the undead, which for some reason is as strong as a chain bolted to the wall. Breaking the bondage is breaking a barrier. It is then, we feel, that we would die, all for breaking the moral rule of the dead: don't come in without invitation.

Knowing of the impasse, I turn. But I do not go away. Not far. I wait. She must leave soon. I will dig my own grave in this very ground if I have to, just so I have satisfaction before I go deeply into the night, and never come out again to live in the mortal world!

18

Descent

I have walked away with the scent of blood. It's how I define my thirst for vengeance, for it is all over me. But what is my vengeance about? Yes, it's about tearing my pain. It's more than jealousy. It's vengeance against the wound, against the thorn that pricked my soul. That thorn is the image of that woman. If she goes, I'll be free! The path will be clear.

Something is happening to my mental state that it is terrifying even to me. I never felt like this. All my moral rectitude—or what I tried to achieve—is now in pieces. But is moral rectitude about enduring pain? Letting it eat you, suck the purpose of your existence? Is it to let someone else be the vampire, one that sucks the blood of your soul? What rights do the dead have? Is it to linger in the back while life goes on without you?

Perhaps I've lost my bearings. I can't help *but* to feel. If I could tear the pain, I would. Even the dead have impossibilities. Pain turns you a demon when the last purpose—the last piece of your sentient existence—is torn from you.

It's for this reason that I wait. For what, I don't know. But I wait.

I wait and wait.

I do, thoughtlessly. The action is mechanical. I'm not the driver of my soul.

The wait might not be long for the dead, for I see 1 am arrive almost as if I had waited twenty minutes. Or, perhaps, occupying myself in pain shortened the space between one point and the other. But it doesn't matter.

My girl is coming out, and her knight in shining armor is walking her to her car. Quite a gentleman! It infuriates me!

I hide in the bushes. What I will do, I know not, but I want to see where she goes. More light enters my eyes as I open them wide with both anger and misery. Now she's going. What will I do? I should be going to Marcus, confront him—show him the shine of my watered down blood-tears.

Instead, I follow her—at first, out of curiosity. Then with vengeance.

Before, I followed like bird of prey. Today, I follow like a hunter, a quiet lioness. I am not myself today.

I follow her almost without thought. I have no thoughts today, yet I know I must stay secret. A secret lioness is no less virulent in her violence just because she is quiet. I don't even think whether this will disqualify me from any vampire court, but I'm not thinking.

She drives far. I don't lose her car even on the freeway. She exits eventually. The first stop she makes is at the light near the gas station where I work. Or perhaps worked. I don't know.

Not far from the gas station is a tobacco shop. After crossing the light, she parks in front of it.

No one around.

When she exits the car, I am near her, though she can't see me. As she puts her keys in her purse, I pick her off the ground.

It is so abrupt, she utters her disbelief.

"What the *fuck!*"

She screams in a panic, as you would if you felt an invisible demon lift you off the ground. I rush forth with her in the air to the back of the gas station, where the bushes are, holding her the way you hold a child to your waist because he won't behave. Unlike a child, she doesn't kick.

Darkness blinds eyes to the ground and other things around except the sky. She doesn't live long enough to warn much of the world. I muffle the last scream she attempts with my fangs over her windpipe. I'm like a lion. And like a lion I suffocate her and when she stops moving I begin to feast on her. It is out of revenge, not hunger. I tear her neck and throat with my fangs, sucking just some of the blood.

I'm not as secret as I think. There is a flashlight. Two flashlights.

"What the fuck!" I hear. "Hey, what are you doing!" It's a loud, alarmed, manly voice. Their light blinds me, but I can sense they are afraid to approach the madness that is I, as if they see a monster and not a woman.

I can imagine what they see as they stand shocked and frozen. A demonic apparition, an animal, red around the mouth with blood, eating the neck of a woman, a woman lying still, wearing a leather jacket, and my eyes fiery red as if gorged with blood.

My flight instinct—my instinct of preservation at this demonic moment—grips me. They might never recognize me if I leave now. As their hands begin to go to the side of their pants, I growl, warn them. I can hear them say, "Get the fuck away!" I could kill them. But I choose otherwise.

I have made my decision and I get up, quickly. I turn and dash away. They come after me in a run, but I soon vanish. I can imagine their frustration and shock at my sudden disappearance.

They must have scoured the entire neighborhood, set dogs on my trail, likely. I know there will be reports. News in the channels. Tomorrow, I am telling myself, I will go to work. That's all. Because I'm too angry to quit. Too angry to let her win. Marcus is mine, and he shall be mine, always.

My black neighbor sees me at the door. He suddenly asks, trying at politeness, "how are you doing?" pausing a moment before he walks away. I look at him a moment, foolish me, then quickly look away. He must have seen something, because he takes a step back. But whatever he saw, he likely cannot imagine. "Are you okay?" he asks, nevertheless. This time I reply, "Yes, goodnight."

He doesn't press. He's too shocked or too polite to probe, or too disliking of me to care enough. Once I enter my apartment, there isn't much to clean. Nothing much to wipe out except around my mouth, and that is done quickly in the sink.

It is too early for me to go into my box, so I spend the evening watching the news. There certainly are several reports about the poor woman whose life I just ended. I don't know what to think. I've become a monstrosity. But I care little for what I did. I just did my job, what any other animal would do who was protecting its territory and property. I'm too used to ending lives to see it as anything but a something similar to clearing a table of bed crumbs. But mortals care.

They make big news out of it. They call the woman's death, "horrific."

I wonder what Marcus is thinking, if he is awake, watching the news. Hopefully he will forget about it. And the sooner, the better. I am not competing again. He is mine, forever. He vowed it. He is wearing the ring of eternity!

19

The Crumbling

I feel sorry for last night. What if this girl was only a playfellow for the times I wasn't around? But no. I am thinking like a vampire. Vampires play these games without feeling a true sense of love or loss when that love ends. Would I indeed clasp a man's hand like that, kiss him sweetly like that—so sickeningly sweetly—when Marcus was not around, if that man was only a playfellow? And if such a man was that and only that, who says that it wouldn't turn to love?

I conjure up as many excuses for killing Marcus' daytime happiness as for feeling sad. But what is done is done. I go to Marcus's house that night, calling work to see if I still have a job. My boss wants to know if everything is okay, and expresses the obvious fact that I've missed too many days. I reply that I am sick, and that I might need to see the doctor in the morning. Then the deal breaker. He tells me to bring him the doctor's note when I get back.

I guess I don't have a job anymore.

I drive, wanting to appear normal again. I find a place to park about a block away from Marcus's place and walk. My somatic senses tell me the night is chilly. As I turn the corner, however, I see police cars. Cops are on his porch. Marcus is telling them about the broken window. How they connected the woman to his place, I don't' know.

But cops have their way.

I choose not to listen to their conversation. I fear to know what Marcus says, as if that would be another cause of pain. I turn and get back to my car. I sit at the steering wheel and think. It's still early and I need something to occupy my mind. I drive to work.

The drive takes me to the scene of the crime. There are police cars at the gas station. I'm impressed at how much ground they've covered in such a short time. Maybe I should become a cop, one who works only at night. That would teach me so much.

I drive home.

I almost veer in direction of Trevor's mansion since it is still early and I might make it home before sunrise. Yet, as I begin to turn, I change my mind and keep going straight. I feel like I've done something that would not sit well with Trevor's court. It would seem like it's a court of death, yet its members don't engage in flights of passion like I did. To lie to them would likely dishonor me and close the door on any membership I aspired to. The court has built a wall of nobility around it, part of which demands self-control, the lack of which threatens the secrecy of the court and its members.

I try to reassure myself that I will be fine. Maybe acknowledging my weakness would go a long way. It might at least keep my honorary membership intact. Yet it's not even a membership at all. I'm an "honorary invitee," meaning I can partake of their society as long as Trevor approves, but I cannot take too much of their blood.

When I get home, I see police cars. My black neighbor is talking to a policeman, pointing in direction of my apartment. I drive away and stop in a dark street. I lock the doors and become invisible. I sit for an hour as if I didn't exist. Then I leave my car and fly to the building. I could effectively remain concealed, except that I have to use my key to enter the complex's door—since I'm not invited in unless I use a key. A police car is still in the parking lot. Something tells me they are waiting for me. I don't know how long they'll wait, but I return to my car. How long will *I* have to wait?

11 o'clock. The police car is still there. I'm so glad dawn is far away. I would have solace if I had my own sleeping box in Trevor's mansion, but such are expressly for members and their concubines. I'm a consort to none. Even my friendship with Trevor does not provide me one. I would have to walk in arm in arm with Henry Tubald or any other member to have those rights. Would Henry even accept a consort escaping from the law—at least one suspected in a crime?

With my love for Marcus it would be impossible to succumb to anyone who did not have my heart. I am completely paralyzed. Nowhere to go at the moment, and Marcus is becoming more distant. Even if he accepts me again, it would be temporary—unless I talk him out of moving to Tennessee for that job offer.

I suddenly become depressed. Roadless.

3 o'clock. Finally, no police car. I enter the complex as I always do and climb the steps to the third floor. Once at home, I want to drink. I look into the cupboard. All my drinks are nearly gone. How could an alcoholic spirit live on such morsels? With all the weight in me—my decision to hide and wait for the hours to go by—I forgot to go to the liquor store. Now it is too late. I must do with what I have.

The next night, I go to Marcus again. I fly there this time. I am invisible as I look through the window.

Marcus is sitting on the bed, the heels of his hands on his eyes as if he was very tired. I materialize and knock on the window. He reacts as if surprised, or stunned, as if I scared him witless. His eyes are red. Either he's grieving or is way too tired. But he gives me a look I've never seen. It is one of anger, as if he just saw an enemy.

Then it changes as he looks at the floor. He is confused, I can tell. He gives me a little smile and a little wave, both so small I wonder if they are what they appear. He looks at the floor again, then at me again. He raises his index finger, asking me to wait.

The ring of eternity is not on his finger.

I wait a little longer than normal, like he is doing something of importance he needs to do before he lets me in. It is a little more than a minute before he lets me in, which he usually does in seconds. I see he has washed his eyes. I see some moisture around them not completely toweled away.

"Hey, sweetheart," I say. I begin to kiss him, but he stops me short. "What's wrong?" I ask.

"How are you doing?" he asks, turning from me, not even answering my question.

"What is wrong?" I ask again. I feel confronted.

"What do you mean? I'm just going to make some coffee. Want some?"

"Eh...sure. But I thought..."

He pauses to look at me. "What did you think?"

"I don't know. I thought we'd...go out or something."

"Go out," he says, nodding with pursed lips. "Right. We can...have coffee first. We can talk, perhaps."

"Sure. I don't have much to say, honestly, other than...well, you know," I reply.

"I see," he says.

"My life is boring."

"How are things at work?" he asks.

"I've been off a couple of days. I've been sleeping. I've been sick."

"Graveyard is hard. You should look for something in the daytime."

"I don't operate well in the day, as I said before."

He brews the coffee. I can smell the richness of the grounds. Marcus is a coffee drinker and will drink coffee anytime. We sit at the kitchen across each other.

"Do you remember when we used to toast with coffee?" he asks.

"Oh, that was so long ago," I say.

"Yes. By the way, did I see you here last night?" He changes the subject, abruptly.

"I don't know. Did you?"

"That's totally evasive!" He is sharp but not loud. "I thought I saw you, and then I saw you disappear. Then a rock came through my window."

"Would someone have a reason to do that?" I ask.

"Maybe yes, maybe no," he replies.

Excellent answer, I think. True and non-committal. And evasive.

"Forget about last night," I say. "The world moves on. If you thought you saw something strange, that was last night. I find it beautiful that we are bound together forever." I reach for his hand and begin to mesh my fingers with his, the same way his lover was doing last night.

"Your hands are cold!" he exclaims, retrieving his hand, not even allowing a full meshing of fingers to happen. Yes, my hands are cold, but something tells me it wasn't the cold that caused him to pull away.

I try to take it lightly.

"I'm sorry," I say. "But you can warm them. It is beautiful to have you, forever." I put my hand on his. He pulls it away, gets up, and goes to the refrigerator. He opens it and looks for something as I watch. Then he closes it, and turns to look at me, leaning against the refrigerator door. He shakes his head.

"We can't do this, anymore," he says.

"Do what?" I ask.

"This...this thing. I love you so much. But I'm tired of the night."

"I cannot come to you in the daytime," I reply. "But it doesn't matter. We are bound, forever!"

He looks at his finger.

"You should wear your ring. You will live eternally, as long as you never take it off," I say.

"I took it off today," he answers. "I needed to wash my hands."

"You can't do that when you are a hundred years old, because you might die."

Now he really looks at me, his eyebrows high, in full skeptic mode.

"Will you live a hundred years to stay with me that long?" he asks.

"I will live, forever," I reply.

"Where is your ring?"

"I don't need one."

"You're that special, ha?" He almost scoffs.

"I am. I don't need one," I repeat.

"I see. Well, I know I will love you forever," he says.

"That's what I need to hear," I reply.

"But...I'm sorry. I want a proper girlfriend. A wife. Children. I...I need a break. We can't just be nighttime lovers. I'm sorry."

It takes me a moment to process what I'm hearing.

"A break?" I exclaim. "A break from me? How long?"

"We'll see how it goes. I...I love you but...I need a break. A long break."

I killed his daytime lover so that we could be together without anyone in between, seeing as we are bound forever. But now he tells me he wants a break? Did she have to stay alive for us to continue? I don't think he can see my anger, or he'd run away—I am sure of that. Had there been no lover, I would have been more understanding, and I would have been sad and heartbroken, but this "break" comes with betrayal, even if the source of it is dead!

"I can't let you go," I say.

"It's just a break," he says. "Even lovers need a time away."

"We don't need a time away."

"You say we are bound, forever. What gives a little break?"

"How long is this break?" I ask again.

"We'll see," he says again.

"I can't accept that. I...I just can't. You promised to be with me, forever! You gave me your vow, in front of people!"

He looks at me.

"I need a break," he says.

20

The Break

We do this dance a little, and it just raises my fury. I am pulsating with anger. Unable to be heartbroken because of the betrayal, and because it didn't help killing the source of it, I am becoming a monster. There is only one way he can be with me, forever, without the ring. I will lose my Marcus, the human, the love of my life, whom I wanted as the love also of my death.

It wouldn't matter to tell him the truth now of what I did. Once he becomes eternal like me, he'll love me, regardless. I am preparing myself for that.

My fangs touch the upper lip of my mouth. The blood from his lover, joined with that of others, feeds the tangibility. They push out my lip, just as Marcus turns his back to me.

"Do you love someone else?" I ask, now hissing.

He doesn't look at me. Doesn't answer a moment.

"I just need a break," he says again.

A chain, intangible but powerful, keeps me in my seat, just as I am about to spring on him like a cat. It's like when angry during a road rage, you want to hit the car in front of you, but you measure the future consequences.

I'm suddenly afraid of destroying the hope. Best to give it time, I think. Best to give it time. All this while my anger has possessed me and built up a pressure that almost makes me explode.

"I must go," I say. "Go, now!"

I don't even give him time to turn fully when I'm out the door. The last time I see him he is out on the porch, looking about, wondering where I've gone.

So close to turning back, but I keep going. I was so close—as he faced the refrigerator—from taking his eternal love by force, by fang. Should I turn back, would I hesitate again? But the Marcus I love in life I want to love in death. That's why I gave him the ring!

It is so precious, his life, his warmth. His betrayal was my fault. I must be understanding. As I get home and sit on my small red couch this time under the dim lights, I reflect and begin to forgive. But jealousy still tugs at me. I hate to lose. Even if the girl—his warm-blooded lover—is dead, I feel I am still competing with her. To renounce him out of love would be losing to her.

I put my face in my hands and cry.

Oh, Phillip! I was a child in my ignorance! You promised me love, happiness and adventure in my dormant state! I even thought, under the hypnosis of your eyes and your world and the words you gave me, that I would love it! Now transformed, I can't go back! Oh, give me back me! Give me back me! Give me the cure! Why did I listen to that hypnosis? Why did I answer to that beautiful view? Oh, give me back me!

I cannot ask for advice. Trevor would not understand. Reminders of his prior warnings ring in my ears. He cannot be right. But the war is not over. I've given it another chance. I just have to think out of the box. Perhaps out of the wooden box in my closet.

As I go over many things in my head, I don't know for how long, there is suddenly a loud knock on my door. I would normally open the door for packages—I get dresses and trinkets, and other things at night—but the knock is too sure and demanding to come from a delivery driver.

When someone requests such an invitation to enter in such a way, it requires a little less than material presence to investigate its driver and purpose. I reduce myself into nothing and pull open the curtain. There, I squeeze my massless essence through the little pores in the pane to the other side.

There are two police cars in the parking lot. What are they doing here? I can't imagine what it could be. It couldn't be about the girl I killed, there is no way I could have been recognized. Perhaps they're just here to ask questions, since the body was found in the back of the gas station, and I work at the gas station. I think.

I pull myself back in and go to the door. I push my head out. Two cops outside. One of them is handsome. Strong. Beautiful blue eyes. The blond hair of his youth is still on him. He'd be a marvelous creature in my arms. Jealousy has a vengeful, destructive brain. Hurt has a way of wanting to sink the last shreds of sanity into the rotten ground.

What have I left? The savior of my life wants to put me back in the grave, threatening to leave me—and I'm supposed to understand, understand that he's alive and that I am dead! Hard to do. Hard to do.

I sniff the young one's cologne. For a cop, he's got good taste. It's Aqua. Is he going out after this? After he puts the handcuffs on me? My heart beats with jealousy and a desire for revenge. Oh, sweet young, strong flesh, put the handcuffs on me and let's go to bed! Turn up the furnace in my dead body. Make me forget!

I return to my room. They're insistent and are already saying the magic words.

"Police!"

I open the door. I've already smelled the handsome cop and we make eye contact. He seems to feel my eye and its enchanting arrows. He becomes utterly polite.

Oh, he wants information about the body found near at gas station. I answer his questions and let him inside.

"Mind if I close the door?" I say. "The draft. It's too cold."

"We rather you leave it open but...just don't lock it," my pretty cop says.

The other cop, an older one, is the business type.

"Ma'am," he says, looking at some papers in his hands. There are questions in it. "Were you at work two nights ago?"

"I was not," I answer.

"Mind telling us where you were around 4 am?"

"I was here, sleeping. I was ill."

"Sorry to hear that," says my little young cop.

"It happens," I respond.

"We have reports that you were seen walking into your door at around 4:30 am."

"Must have been the time I came out to the balcony. I'm still awake around that time. Your internal clock changes when you work graveyard."

"It does," says my handsome cop, nodding.

They ask me a few other questions. My answers, if the smile of my handsome cop is any revealing, clear me. I tell them I don't mind them coming back for a follow-up, and that next time I might offer them coffee, if they don't mind drinking it.

"Not when we're working, when we're in uniform," says my pretty cop.

I check myself before asking when he should come out of it. It would make me look like a classless woman. Only men can get away with being so trashy. Although I've seen women get away with much, and men with little. Though, looking back at this little episode, it would have been classless to ask when he should come out of his uniform then—but not after we had been alone and been playful. Though there are all types of people, even dead ones. What the goose does is not appreciated by the gander, and so forth.

"What do you think?" says my handsome cop to the other. I have followed them to their car.

"She sounds innocent," says his colleague.

"The private guards say they recognized her."

"She doesn't look like a mad woman," says the older cop.

"No, she doesn't. Unless she's a great actress."

"You never know."

"How old did she look to you? Like twenty-one, twenty-two?"

"Why? You like her?"

"If she is innocent, why not?" says the young cop.

"Yeah, she's beautiful, I gotta give her that," the older cop replies.

Once they get into their car and leave, I know this isn't over. But I'm not afraid. I have suffered dying too much to care about what life brings to my nonexistence within the material world. For you see, though you can see me, I'm nonexistent. I'm an apparition. Though I materialize into something tangible, I've ceased existing.

The dead need rest from trouble and worry, and they don't truly worry, unless they attach too many things of value near the heat, such as I have. For I have placed my heart into the hands of one whose life brings it meaning. But the rest does not matter. The rest cannot touch me. I am a spirit. I am immortal. Nothing can truly touch me except in my heart. The moment Marcus dies, the spell is broken. I will be truly dead. Uncaring. A true animal.

Should I turn him, would I love him as much? I love the Marcus of now. Would I love the Marcus of then? The Marcus I loved then would not be the Marcus I love now. Such a person would be gone. He would be a past. He might have to pretend, like me, to be alive, but he would be, for most intents and purposes, just an apparition, and apparitions are nonexistent material beings, for they only take for themselves what they need to take before going their way into thin air, as if they were never there. We come and disappear, and care little for the feelings of others, except through a sense of honor still left in us, as I believe.

21

The Final Revenge

I don't know why I don't go to Marcus the next few nights. In part, I *do* know. It's one of those moments when knowledge and ignorance become blurred. The last night of my wondering and thinking about solutions to solve the problem of my dead existence without Marcus, I arrive at an answer.

I will reclaim my place within Trevor's court and my relationship with Marcus. I have to keep both. I close my eyes. The feeling is both cruel and sweet. Painful and yet enchanted with dreams and possibilities.

That evening of all evenings, my mother calls me. She doesn't bring back the fact that I left so suddenly from her house a few nights ago.

For some reason, she is a welcome call. I feel like telling the world what I'm going to do—of the joy that will happen once that thing is done.

"Hey sweetie, how are you doing?" she starts.

"I love you, Mother," I say. "I miss being with you." This I say coldly, but I mean it. I miss my old life. To her ears, it sounds both beautiful and strange.

"Oh, sweetheart! I love to hear you say that. I love you too. But why so tragic? Is everything okay?"

"I am what I am. Sorry I can't be with you."

I don't know if this makes sense to her, but I'm thinking so many things.

"You are what you are. That's a strange thing to say. But I know you are what you are. A lovely person with a big heart. And I know I always bother you about visiting me. But don't worry. I know you've been distracted with Marcus. He's such a nice man. He always waited for you, hoping you'd return. I hope everything is well with him?"

"Everything is...dandy. Today we're going to be together, forever."

"Really? What does that mean? You're getting married?"

"In a sort of way. No ceremony."

"Well, when you get *truly* married, there needs to be one, and I need to be there. We all do. We all love you and miss you."

"I love you and miss you all, too. But I have to go, now. We will talk later. Goodbye, Mother."

When I hang up, I feel my anger boiling again. Mother's talk of marriage reminded me suddenly of the vow Marcus made, which he threw away at first glance of a woman.

Or was it a first glance?

After wondering all last night before the sun started poking its head into the curtains whether I've been a fool—and thinking that a death with Marcus would be better than a life without him—I decided to take my feared step.

He's free in the daytime. He could trip and fall again onto another woman, have a child, a family, and completely abandon me then. How many women will I have to kill?

And then the children! Think of the children!

As to giving him freedom, he did not let *me* be free! He wrapped his heart around mine, possessed me, in life and in death. But how much has he loved her? I know he was crying for her the last time I saw him. I know he knew what had happened to her, and probably blames me for it. Will he renounce me for it? It's either happiness or a darkness that I fear in death without him.

I make myself pretty. Deliciously pretty. Put on makeup. Put on my prettiest dress. A rose over my ear. I put on high heels. I've been neglecting my looks the last few days, and perhaps that has salted the worm. Today, he will be mine. He will desire me. He will come willingly into my arms, into the embrace of my fangs.

Oh, look at me! I never looked so pretty before!

I put on a fine Dolce & Gabanna perfume behind my ears, spray it lightly over my clothes, and I vanish into thin air. The moon is shining bright, a true pearl, and it is before his window. It glints silver fire around the edges, as a cloud, trying to cover it, gets shamed. In all her glory, madam moon shines through, breaking through the cloud.

It is two o'clock. He will hear my knock. As I travel to his house, several patrol cars streak by, sirens waling. I'm still curious of many things. I stop to hear, out of curiosity, what some people say on the street.

"I heard the body was stolen," a man tells a woman.

"Stolen?" The woman seems shocked.

"That's why they're going in such a hurry," the man says.

They quickly change the subject. I do not care. I keep going. Going to my love. To possess him, forever. Where shall we go? We shall go to Gibraltar. Make sweet love under the moon in a secluded island, maybe over the ocean's waters. Nothing to stop us! We will sleep in catacombs and kill those who dare disturb us. Or maybe that might not be possible. We'll just rent a hotel room.

As I arrive, knitting dreams, possibilities even in death, I am smiling. All these things can be possible. Once mine, forever.

Once mine, forever.

I turn, turn away. Away from the window. In pain. I seek a fire to dive into, a barrel full of garlic and stakes.

Marcus will never be mine!

I have failed!

The moon does not shine on him and me, but on him and *her*.

I still see her through my heart's tears—her arms around him, her fangs on him—he paling, sinking into her power, into her love, blending his heart with hers.

Did you hear the cry? It made the moon rush behind a cloud. I fell to the ground, trembling. What is it that makes spirits tremble? Unable to shed mortal tears, sweet salty tears, I reach for the trickle on my face. It's blood now! It's blood!

No point staying longer, suffering the torment, waiting for the sun to finish me.

I knocked on the window, he did not hear me. She kept going with her love and her malice. I screamed, my heart screamed, my eternity screamed! He did not stir from her arms, did not turn to look at me as she drained every drop of his mortal life, every drop of his essence, every drop of his blood!

I leaned my forehead on the pane, crying and knocking. I was unable to get in to rescue him—to rescue me! I could not penetrate that wall!

If the spirit can cry, if hearts can shed tears, if hope can be so utterly broken, I was a fine portrait of that.

I was there for whoever happened by, though I doubt there was anyone around. Only the moon. The coward moon!

I thought I had killed her—perfectly killed her! Yet I failed in that. It was those flashlights! It was my escape! I did not bury the fatal stake in her body!

I never meant to turn her. I meant to end her! But I killed her, imperfectly. She hates me. I am her enemy, and she has come to take revenge, surely knowing, or surely feeling, that I was more than a boy's night-dream! Now Marcus, my beautiful Marcus, belongs to her. He is her consort. Her partner. Her blood-love.

I go home to cry. As I try to make sense of it all, a knock.

Here he is, the pretty cop. I take the revenge of consolation. I put him under a spell and give him the embrace of my fangs. His blood runs down my chin. All this while his colleague checks for evidence of the crime in all my drawers, which I've instructed him to do.

My handsome cop's name is Byron. He is pale by the time he gets back to his partner. He is also weak and needs to go home. I know where he lives, now. I will knock on his window tomorrow night. Slowly is the best way to make an eternal lover. Phillip taught me well.

But I still think of Marcus. I still think of recovering him from the clutches of the *brunette evil-tress*, whose name I still don't know. I will arm myself with a stake, and when I see her...

But now I must cry, cry now that Byron is gone. Cry like vampires cry, with the pain of a thousand tombs. And with blood.

The End

About the author

Maxime Norrvik is the author of *The Passion of the Immortals* and the forthcoming novel *Other Gods*. A lifelong storyteller, he began writing at the age of six, driven by a desire so strong that he learned to read just to bring his own tales to life.

Born with an affinity for the gothic and the fantastic, Norrvik draws inspiration from classic works like *Dracula*, blending supernatural intrigue with deep explorations of human emotion. His stories blur the line between reality and the unreal, weaving intricate narratives where the extraordinary feels tangible and the mundane brims with magic.

Beyond writing, Norrvik is a musician and an avid chess player. His time in Australia, where he is a proud father to a young daughter, has further shaped his perspective, enriching his characters with a strong sense of place and humanity.

Through both prose and character, Norrvik delves not only into the extraordinary but also into the raw, complex emotions that define his characters' inner lives.

www.ingramcontent.com/pod-product-compliance
Lightning Source LLC
Chambersburg PA
CBHW030427310726
48979CB00009B/1658/J

* 9 7 8 0 6 4 8 4 3 4 9 3 1 *